What *was* it about him?

Ed was just an ordinary man—wasn't he? So he was good-looking—so were lots of men. Jo pulled out one of the chairs from under the table and sat down, giving her tea very much more attention than it really merited while she waited for her head to clear. He didn't help matters. He flipped the chair round, straddling it and resting his forearms on the back, the mug dangling from long, strong fingers.

Ridiculous. Even his fingers drove her crazy!

Caroline Anderson's nursing career was brought to an abrupt halt by a back injury, but her interest in medical things led her to work first as a medical secretary and then, after completing her teacher training, as a lecturer in Medical Office Practice to trainee medical secretaries. She lives in rural Suffolk with her husband, two daughters and assorted animals.

Recent titles by the same author:

SARAH'S GIFT
CAPTIVE HEART
DEFINITELY MAYBE

AN UNEXPECTED BONUS

BONUS

BY

CAROLINE ANDERSON

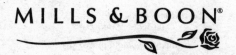

MILLS & BOON®

First published in Great Britain 1999
Harlequin Mills & Boon Limited,
Eton House, 18-24 Paradise Road, Richmond, Surrey TW9 1SR

© Caroline Anderson 1999

ISBN 0 263 81521 8

Set in Times Roman 10½ on 11½ pt.
03-9904-50866-D

Printed and bound in Norway
by AIT Trondheim AS, Trondheim

CHAPTER ONE

'HE'S gorgeous!'

Jo looked down at the baby girl in her arms and smiled. 'Mmm—but he's a she.'

Sue propped her arms on the edge of the crib and laughed softly. 'Not the baby, idiot. *Him.* Our Dr Latimer.'

'Oh, him. He's come in, has he? Such dedication to duty on New Year's Day.' Jo laid the baby down on her side, covered her up and straightened. 'I was just tucking up our first baby of the year. I nearly missed her arrival—in a bit of a hurry, weren't you, sweetheart?'

The baby ignored her, and so did Sue.

'You ought to see him—six foot something, dark hair, laughing grey-blue eyes...'

'Sounds like a cliché.'

Sue gave an exasperated sigh. 'Look, Jo, he's perfect. Just what you need—'

'Whoa there! Steady on.' Jo stopped what she was doing and met her friend's eyes. 'What I need,' she pointed out carefully, 'is calm, stability, security—'

'Fun, laughter, a social life—'

'A pension—'

'Pension!' Sue exploded. 'Why do you need a pension? You're twenty-nine!'

'Thirty—and because, as I've just proved, I'm getting older.'

Sue made a rude noise and bent over the baby. 'Hi, sweetheart. Welcome to the world of pensions and premature ageing. It'll be your birthday next week at this rate, you wait and see.'

Jo swatted her with the file and went out into the corridor, hiding her grin. 'You're impossible. I'm not interested in Dr Latimer. For all we know he could be married…'

'Uh-uh. Single—not even divorced.'

'So why's he taken a job in a quiet little seaside town in Suffolk? He's probably got totally unacceptable habits, or halitosis.'

Sue followed her down the corridor to the nursing station. 'No halitosis…'

'And of course you got close enough to find out.'

'Oh, yes. Matron introduced us. I swear, if I wasn't already married…' She paused. 'He's lovely, Jo, really.' Her eyes grew serious. 'He is. You wait till you meet him. He could be Mr Right.'

'I'm sure he is—for someone, but that someone isn't me, Sue. I don't believe in happy ever after.'

Sue propped herself against the wall and watched as Jo dropped the file back into the trolley. 'So have an affair.'

Jo laughed. 'In Yoxburgh? Got any more good ideas?'

'I mean it. It's time you got out and had a bit of fun. I think it's amazing that you're as normal as you are, the life you lead. You're closeted up like a nun—and what about Laura? Is she going to grow up thinking that men are a bad idea and living alone is the norm?'

Jo shook her head in disbelief and turned towards her friend.

'Leave it, Sue, please. Laura and I are fine. We don't need anyone else. I know you're only trying to help, but we're quite happy the way we are.'

Sue shrugged. 'Have it your own way.'

'I will. We're fine.' Jo sighed inwardly. It wasn't a

lie. They were happy, more or less. Sometimes they were happier than others, but most of the time they rubbed along all right, and if there were nights sometimes when the bed seemed cold and empty—well, they were few and far between, and she had plenty of friends to pass the time with.

She didn't admit to herself that passing the time was all she did, putting one foot in front of the other, taking the days one at a time, shuffling on towards retirement and the hereafter with little enthusiasm for anything but Laura and the mums and babies in her care—

Lord, how maudlin!

'Stop matchmaking, Sue,' she told her friend firmly. 'Anyway, haven't you got anything better to do?'

'Oh, tons—all my PNs. You can tell me what you think of him later. See you!'

Jo watched her go despairingly. She had a few post-natal checks to do herself, but first of all, since Dr Latimer was in the building, he could make himself useful.

She quickened her stride, bustling down the corridor towards the entrance, and as she rounded the corner she almost fell over a group of people standing clustered in Reception.

Matron, the receptionist, a nursing sister—and him. At least, she imagined it was him—and, yes, he was gorgeous, she supposed, if your taste ran to that sort of thing.

Tall, dark, handsome, clichéd—the stuff of fiction. As far as Jo was concerned, though, he was just a man like all the others.

Then he looked at her, those storm-grey eyes meeting hers and holding, and, like a display of baked beans in a supermarket, she felt as if someone had yanked out a tin from the bottom row and tumbled her into a heap at his feet.

'Ah, Jo—perfect timing.'

She blinked, breaking the spell, and looked away. To her astonishment she was still standing, rather puzzled by the strange hiccup in her heart rate and the fizzing in her veins.

Not because of him, surely? Men just didn't do that to her!

Matron smiled, holding out her arm to welcome her to the group. 'This is Jo Halliday—she's the senior community midwife. You'll be seeing a lot of her, of course, because she runs the antenatal clinics in your surgery as well as the classes here. Jo, come and meet Ed Latimer.'

Come and meet him? She might, if she tried really hard, be able to remember how to walk!

'Hi, there,' she said, thankful that her voice at least sounded normal. 'Pleased to meet you. Actually, I've got a job for you, if I could hijack you from the grand tour?'

'Oh, we've finished,' Matron said airily. 'He's all yours.'

He chuckled, a deep, rich sound that for some reason sent a shiver down her spine. 'At your service,' he said with a little bow of his head, and the grin that accompanied it made her heart do something crazy and stupid and not entirely normal. 'What did you want me for?'

She wasn't sure any longer. Her body seemed to have a hidden agenda all its own. She swallowed. 'New baby needs a check—I wonder if you'd do the honours.'

'Sure. Lead the way.'

She did, taking him back down the corridor towards the GP unit, aware with every step of his presence at her side.

'Here we are, female infant of Angela Grigson, born at eight-thirty this morning.'

'So, little baby Grigson is the first of the New Year?'

'Yes. It's a small unit, so it's amazing we've had one on New Year's Day. Sometimes it's days before we get a baby—last year it was the ninth of January.'

'Normal vaginal delivery, I take it? Was she booked for admission to the GP unit?'

'No. She was due to go to the hospital, it's only her first, but she didn't have time. I was hardly here myself! I've checked everything except the heartbeat, but I expect you'll want to check her again.'

She was running on like a steam train! She shut her mouth with a little snap and stepped back.

Ed Latimer gave her a quizzical little look, then turned his attention to the peaceful baby. 'OK. Sorry, little one, I'm going to wake you up.' He looked round. 'Where's Mum?'

'Gone to the loo. She's very relaxed about it all.'

'Not to mention hasty! What was the Apgar score?'

'Ten,' she replied promptly, glad to focus on the professional rather than the general. 'She was very alert and vocal at birth, bright pink and flailing furiously!'

'Excellent. No other problems, I take it, apart from the unseemly speed?'

'No, everything was perfectly normal, just fast. Mum had the shakes afterwards, but that's quite common with hasty deliveries.'

Jo watched him undress the tiny scrap, his big hands astonishingly gentle, his eyes scanning the baby for anything out of the ordinary. He checked the eyes, the ears, the mouth and nose, the fontanelles or soft spots on the head, both hands and feet, all the digits, then laid the baby face down over his palm and checked the spine with a big, blunt fingertip.

Then he checked her bottom to make sure that all necessary organs were present and correct, dropped her an inch onto the cot to test her Moro reflex and grunted in satisfaction as the baby flung her arms out and cried. She grasped his fingers and held on as he lifted her, and when he dangled her so her feet just touched the mattress she tried to walk.

'Good girl. Now the bit you'll hate. Sorry, poppet.' He folded her little legs up, bent them up against her sides and wiggled them to check her hip joints.

Predictably she wailed, and he scooped her up and hugged her. 'Sorry, little one,' he murmured, cradling her against his chest. Just to get her revenge, she emptied her bladder down his shirt.

'Well, that answers that question,' he said with a grimace. 'Her waterworks function.'

Jo laughed and, taking the baby from him, she put her into a nappy and laid her back into the cot so he could listen to her heart.

'That'll teach me to hug them when they're naked,' he said ruefully, blotting at his shirt with a paper towel.

'At least she isn't a boy. They always pee in your eye.'

He grinned at her, and once again her heart did that stupid thing.

Nuts.

She watched in silence as he checked the baby's heart for any unusual sounds, and then he folded the stethoscope and tucked it back into his pocket, before dressing the little one again.

'Can you manage?' Jo asked, which earned her a wry look.

'Why do you women think you're the only ones who get to play with the new babies?' he said softly, and turned his attention back to the little one in his hands. 'Can I manage?' he murmured. 'The nerve of the woman! Just so cheeky, isn't she? Yes!'

He was competent, she had to give him that. She wondered if there was a child in his life—or a partner not covered by the standard 'single/married/widowed/divorced' categories of the application form.

Very likely. He was the boy next door grown up, and if he was still single it was very odd.

Perhaps he had unspeakable habits after all?

Then he straightened and met her eyes, and there was something sad and lonely lurking in the depths of them—something that tugged at an echo in her heart. She wanted to reach out to him, to touch him, to ask what it was that made him sad, but before she could make a fool of herself there was a shuffling behind her, and a cheery voice said, 'Hello, there. Everything all right?'

She turned, dragging her eyes from his, and smiled at the young woman in the tatty dressing-gown who climbed up onto the bed and sat down cautiously.

'Hi, Angela. Fine—just a routine check on the baby. How are you feeling now?'

'Oh, fine. Bit sore.' She looked across at Ed and smiled. 'You must be the new doctor.'

'That's me—Ed Latimer. Pleased to meet you. Congratulations on a perfect little baby. I've checked her over and she's all present and correct—lovely. Well done.' He took her hand in a firm grasp, and Angela Grigson turned to putty. She smiled and dimpled and went all silly, and Jo rolled her eyes and looked away.

The woman was happily married and had been for the past five years, and yet one look at their new GP and she went gaga only hours after the birth of her first child.

Jo predicted a massive rush of minor ailments at the surgery in the next few days, checking out the new doctor. The grapevine would be humming like a guitar string and nobody would be able to talk about anything else!

'I told you he'd knock your socks off.'

'He's just a man.'

'Pooh. He's gorgeous.'

'We've done this conversation for the past three days. Can't anyone talk about anything else? I'm getting sick of hearing his name.'

'Whose name?'

They both jumped guiltily and turned towards the door of the surgery kitchen. 'Yours,' Jo said, not bothering to lie. 'Everyone in Yoxburgh is talking about you—and it's only Monday. You're the sole topic of conversation!'

He gave a short laugh. 'I hope it's good.'

'So far you don't seem to have irritated the dowagers or killed off their grandchildren so, yes, at the moment it's good. You might blow it yet, of course, once you start doing a few more surgeries.'

He laughed. 'Quite probably.' He propped his lean hips against the worktop and looked hopefully at the kettle. 'Any chance of a cup of tea?'

Sue scooted through the door. 'I'm off on my visits. Jo'll make you tea—she's the resident mummy.'

He quirked a brow. 'Resident mummy?'

Jo laughed a little awkwardly and flicked the button on the kettle. 'I make them look after themselves and eat properly, and I nag a bit.'

'You sound like an asset to the practice.'

She laughed again. 'They hate it, mostly—except when I'm dishing out tea and coffee. Then they usually form an orderly queue.'

He chuckled and reached for two mugs from the rack, handing them to her. 'Is it just us?'

'At the moment. Were you looking for me, or just the kettle?'

'You, actually.' He lounged against the worktop again, looking sexier than he had any right to. 'I wanted to go over the routine—you know I'm taking over all the obstetrics for the practice?'

'Yes, I did. Not a problem—we can sit down with our tea and go through it all. It's quite straightforward.'

'Have you got time?'

'Just about. I'm on call but it's quiet at the moment. How about you?'

He chuckled. 'I'm on half-timetable this week, just while I settle in. They wanted me to have a nice gentle introduction so I didn't get the screaming ab-dabs and run off into the sunset before I'd had time to get used to the place. It's quite a luxury, really, after doing locum work for six months and my GP training and obstetrics before that, but I must confess to being a bit bored.'

'It won't last,' she assured him drily. 'With this flu epidemic and the worst part of the winter lined up, you can be sure it'll deteriorate very soon.'

'I'm so glad. I was beginning to wonder if I'd have enough to do or if it was all a big mistake.'

Jo gave an astonished laugh. 'Just make the most of it,' she advised him with a grin. 'How do you take your tea?'

'White, no sugar—thanks.' His fingers brushed hers as he took the mug, and a shiver of something elemental and thoroughly silly ran up her arm and curdled her brain.

What *was* it about him? He was just an ordinary man—wasn't he? So he was good-looking—so were lots of men. She pulled out one of the chairs from under the table and sat down, giving her tea very much more at-tention than it really merited while she waited for her head to clear. He didn't help matters. He flipped the chair round, straddling it and resting his forearms on the back, the mug dangling from long, strong fingers.

Ridiculous. Even his fingers drove her crazy!

'So, tell me about how the obstetrics is arranged,' he said suddenly, dragging her back to earth. 'How many of our mums have their babies here and how many in the Audley?'

She latched onto the professional conversation like a lifeline and launched into a barrage of statistics. 'More and more are having them either here or at home—recently I've had one or two who've given birth at the Audley and gone into the GP unit for a postnatal period of two or three days, just to get a rest.'

'Yes, that's one of the problems of sending them all home so soon—I often wonder if they don't need more rest, but busy hospitals certainly don't seem to be the place to get it.'

She set her mug on the table, folding her arms to keep her fingers still. 'Most of the postnatal cases are mums with other children and just need a break, or their partners aren't able to take time off, but whatever their reasons we encourage them to use the unit, of course, because otherwise we can't justify its existence and it'll be closed.'

'Is that likely?'

She shrugged and pulled a face. 'Maybe. Several units in the Suffolk area have closed over the last ten to twenty years, and others are under threat. We use it for obs and gynae post-op as well as just a straightforward delivery unit to maximise the use of the beds, but it's certainly used to capacity most of the time one way and another and we try and keep it that way.'

He nodded thoughtfully, sipping his tea and gazing absently over the rim of his mug. 'So how many babies are delivered in the community every year?' he asked next, trapping her with his eyes.

Were they grey or blue? Hard to tell in this light...

'In our immediate area about eighty, either in the unit or at home. We refer whenever we feel it's necessary, and we never take chances. We've got fairly strict criteria for the GP unit, although if they don't comply with the criteria I might still let them have a home birth, but we watch them like hawks. We're too far from the specialist unit to be able to take risks.'

His eyes searched hers. 'Does that undermine your confidence?'

She smiled. 'It used to. Not any more. I think experience counts for a lot. I'm much more willing to let mums have a go now than I used to be.'

'Are you happy to rely on your professional judgement, or would you like tighter guidelines?'

'No. I like to be able to take each case on its merits. I rely on instinct as well.' She waited for the criticism, but to her surprise it wasn't forthcoming.

'So do I,' he admitted, 'although I'm not sure I always trust my instincts yet. Maybe when I've got more experience in general practice. In the meantime, I'd rather check with a colleague. I'm not afraid to admit I don't know all the answers.'

'So you won't mind when I keep you in order?' she said with a hesitant smile.

He chuckled. 'I'll be relying on it.'

She nodded, relieved that they agreed about something so important. Not that she'd meant to be so unsubtle about it, but there you go, she thought, not everyone's born to be a diplomat.

Her bleeper warbled, and she popped through to Reception, then came back. 'Got to fly,' she told him, 'one of my imminent mums. In fact, are you busy? I'll need an accomplice—this one's a home birth. You could gain a bit of that experience you were talking about.'

'Sure.' He drained his tea, flipped the chair back under the table and stood, ready and waiting. 'Your car or mine, or both?'

'I'll take mine because it's got my stuff in—you're welcome to hitch a ride or take yours, whatever, but I'll ring her first.'

She went into the office and rang through to Julie Brown, half her attention still on the man lounging on the wall behind her. 'Julie? Hi—Jo Halliday. How's things?'

'Oh, you know—I had a twinge so I finished feeding the sheep and came in, and once I stopped moving I realised things were getting on a bit. I don't think it'll be long.'

'Hang on, then. Is anyone with you?'

'No. Tim's down at the other farm and the kids are with Mum.'

'Right, unlock the back door, shut the dog up and go up to your room. Then lie down and *rest*!'

Julie chuckled. 'Yes, Sergeant-Major, sir!'

'Just do it. I'll be ten minutes.'

She cradled the phone. 'Farmer's wife,' she said to Ed. 'She says it won't be long. She's had two—I believe her. Are you ready? I'm going now.'

He nodded. 'Fine.'

'Are you going to follow? I'll have to stay two hours after the birth.'

'No problem. I've got nothing else to do and it might be useful. I'll come with you, if I may? I can ask you questions on the way.'

And distract me, she thought, but in fact he didn't. He sat very quietly and said not a lot until they'd arrived, and then as they got out she noticed he was a little pale.

'You don't take any prisoners, do you?' he said drily.

'I said we were in a hurry,' she said with a grin, and he managed a wan smile.

'Hmm. I'm not used to being driven. I find it a bit unnerving.'

She laughed, grabbed her bag out of the car and headed round the side of the house. A volley of barking heralded their arrival, and as she opened the back door the big black dog launched itself at her.

'Brogue, get down!'

The dog subsided, licking her hand, and with a frown she went into the kitchen and found Julie slumped over the table. She lifted her head and gazed at Jo.

'Couldn't make the stairs,' she said breathlessly. 'Think it's coming—'

'Good job you've got a decent-sized table in here, then, isn't it, since the floor's a bit doggy?' Jo said with a grin. 'Ed, give me a hand. Oh, Julie, this is Dr Ed Latimer, our new GP obstetrician.'

Julie peered up at him, and said weakly, 'Hi.' She dropped her head again. 'Oh, here we go again...'

'She's having a contraction—come on, let's clear the table and move her as soon as it's over so I can have a look.' Jo scooped papers and mugs off the table, and stacked cushions for Julie to lean against, then glanced at Ed over her shoulder. 'There's a big black box in the boot of my car. Could you get it?'

He went without argument, to her relief, and was back in seconds, by which time she'd shut Brogue in the utility room and was back with Julie.

'Thanks,' she murmured, lifting the lid off the box. Pulling out the delivery pack and a few inco pads, she spread them out on the top of the big old table and they lifted Julie onto it. Her dress was quickly hitched up, and as they dispensed with her underwear it was obvious the baby wasn't waiting for anyone.

'I'll just wash my hands,' Jo said, but there wasn't time to find gloves, because the baby was coming, and coming now. 'Just pant,' Jo told Julie, and the baby shot out into her hands in a slippery rush just moments later.

'Hello, little fellow,' she said with a smile. Lifting him, she put him down on Julie's abdomen and grinned at Ed. 'Three thirty-seven. Remember that. Didn't need us at all,' she added over the baby's indignant squall. Washing her hands again, she dried them on a clean towel from one of the kitchen drawers, put gloves on and checked for any problems.

It all looked very straightforward, and after the cord stopped pulsing she clamped and cut it. Wrapping the baby in another towel from the drawer, she handed him to Ed. 'Hold this,' she ordered.

'This,' he said softly. 'Is that any way to speak to you, son?' he murmured and, taking the corner of the towel, he gently wiped the baby's face.

Jo dragged her eyes away from him and tried to concentrate on the patient and her needs. She was propped on the pile of hastily assembled cushions, and she looked thoroughly uncomfortable on the hard tabletop.

'I'd like to move you to somewhere more comfy,' she was saying, when the back door burst open and Tim erupted into the room, his eyes wild.

'Ah, Julie, love, you could have waited for me!' he said with a laugh, and hugged his wife.

'It's a boy,' she told him, and he closed his eyes and hugged her again.

'Everything all right?'

'Think so,' Jo told him. 'We haven't really had time to check—he's only just been born a few minutes.'

'You check Mum, I'll check the baby,' Ed said, and

she was suddenly reminded that he was a fellow-professional and not just someone she'd dragged along for the ride. She wondered how badly she'd ordered him around, but couldn't remember.

Too bad. The baby was the first priority, and it was her delivery anyway. 'Do you want to wait for the placenta, or shall I give you an injection?' she asked Julie, knowing full well what the answer would be.

'I'll wait—I can feel a contraction now, I think.'

Jo laid a hand on Julie's soft abdomen and pressed down, and she could feel the uterus working. 'Yes, you're right. We'll wait. Are you OK there?'

'I'll manage.'

It didn't take long. She popped the afterbirth into one of the bowls and checked it quickly, filled the other with hot water to wash the mother down, examined Julie for any little nicks or tears and declared her to be fine.

'Baby, too. He's got good lungs,' Ed said ruefully, pulling the earpieces of the stethoscope out of his ears so the bellowing didn't damage his hearing permanently. 'I'll check his heart later when he's quiet but, judging by his colour, I can't imagine he's got a problem.'

'No. He's a lusty little chap,' Jo said, giving him her attention for the first time. She looked at the placenta more thoroughly, lifting up the membranes and checking for any abnormalities, then put it into a yellow clinical waste bag, sealed it and put it inside another one.

'Want to weigh him?' Ed asked.

'Not yet. I want to clear up a little first and then get Julie upstairs. You feeling strong, Tim?' she asked, bagging up the rest of the clinical waste and popping a pad between Julie's legs.

He grinned and scooped his wife up in his arms, carrying her up to their bedroom with the others trailing behind. 'Fancy having him in the kitchen,' Tim said affectionately as he set her down. 'You spend your life at that damn table—I might have known you'd have the baby on it!'

'It'll be something to tell the grandchildren when they come over for Sunday lunch,' Julie said with a chuckle.

'Hmm. Eating off the same table, I have no doubt.' Jo laughed. 'Right, we need to undress you and freshen you up, feed the baby, and then after your bath I think you'll need a rest—I should think you're exhausted after such a hard labour,' she said with a smile.

'Oh, yes—all of about an hour from the first twinge.'

'You should have rung me on the mobile,' Tim scolded.

'I did—you left it switched off,' Julie pointed out.

'Now, now, children, don't fight,' Jo said. She sent Tim off to clear up the devastation in the kitchen and make everyone a cup of tea while she helped Julie out of her clothes and into a dressing-gown.

Once Julie was undressed she was able to feed the baby, and Jo felt the usual surge of satisfaction as she watched the little baby suckle from his mother. He was the third of their children that she'd delivered or monitored in pregnancy, and it was gratifying to have been involved in the arrival of the whole family.

She looked up at Ed, wondering what he was making of all of this, and surprised a look of sadness and longing on his face again. How strange. He was so good with children—had he lost one? Was that it?

He looked up and caught her eye. His expression became immediately neutral, as if he'd carefully schooled his face to remove the traces of emotion.

'Teatime,' Tim said cheerfully, pushing the door open with his foot and carrying in a tray.

Ed stood up. 'Not for me, thanks. Things seem fine. I think I'll go for a wander—have a look round outside.

I'm still feeling a bit green after the white-knuckle ride—Jo doesn't exactly hang about. I'll be back in a while.'

His smile was a little strained. Jo sipped her tea and wondered what had put that look on his face and made him want to run away—because that was what he was doing, she was sure. She didn't believe he was still feeling queasy for a moment.

The baby dozed off, and Julie put her cup down and smiled wearily at Jo. 'I could murder that bath now.'

'Good idea. I'll run it, you stay there.'

It wasn't too hot because of the baby, but she made it nice and deep because there was nothing like a good wallow after delivery. Then she helped Julie into the bath, before unwrapping the baby that Tim was holding and lowering him carefully into the water between Julie's knees.

He woke up a little, blinking in the light and gazing up with those wonderful blue eyes of the newborn, and Julie helped her wash his soft, delicate skin with careful hands.

'He seems so tiny—you forget,' Julie said, her voice hushed and full of awe, and Jo looked at him and remembered Laura.

'You're right—you do forget. I can't believe Laura was ever this small.'

'No. She certainly doesn't look it now. She's so tall, isn't she? How old is she?'

'Twelve. She takes after me and my mother—we're both quite tall.'

Jo scooped the baby out of the water and wrapped him in a towel off the radiator, then sprinkled a few drops of lavender and tea-tree oil into the bath and topped up the hot water. Julie sank down for a good wallow and sighed with ecstasy.

'I can't believe she's twelve,' she said after a moment, sounding stunned. 'Almost a teenager. I can remember when she was born. I don't know how you cope alone.'

'I've got Mum. I couldn't work and look after her without my mother's help.'

Julie laughed. 'No, mums are wonderful. I'd be lost without mine during lambing and harvesting.'

Jo took the baby across the landing to the bedroom, leaving the doors open, and took the little spring balance out of the box Tim had brought upstairs. She hooked the nylon sling underneath it, popped the baby naked into the sling and held up the balance.

'Three point seven kilos—eight pounds three ounces,' she told the mother. 'How does that compare?'

'Heavier than Lucy, about the same as Robert.'

'What are you calling this one? Does he have a name?'

Tim came upstairs again and into the room. 'Michael, we'd thought.'

'Or Anna,' Julie said from the depths of her bath. 'I think Michael's more appropriate. I could kill another cup of tea.'

Tim went through to the bathroom, mug in hand. 'How did I guess?' he said, a smile in his voice, and for the millionth time Jo wondered what it would have been like to have a father for her daughter, a man who loved and cherished her and was committed to her, instead of—

She cut off the train of thought and concentrated on the baby. He was gorgeous, a lovely sturdy little chap with everything going for him. She put a nappy on him before he could catch her out, popped him into a vest and sleepsuit and tucked him up in the crib that was standing ready in the corner.

Then she helped Julie out of the bath, and while Tim

helped her into her nightclothes and down to the warm kitchen Jo went down ahead of them and tidied up her bag, settled herself at the cleaned-up table and wrote up her notes while they sat by the Aga and chatted about the delivery.

Jo lifted her head as Ed came back in, and Tim grinned at him.

'You must have heard the kettle boil. Fancy a cuppa now?'

Ed smiled, and the strain seemed to have left his face. 'Thanks. Don't mind if I do. Everything all right?'

'Yup. No problems.' Jo shut the notes, handed the file back to Julie and slipped her pen back into her pocket, before washing her hands again. 'Baby's upstairs in the bedroom if you want to check his heart now he's quiet.'

'Sure. Thanks.'

He came down a few minutes later, the baby in his arms, and handed him to Julie. 'He was chewing his fists and grizzling—I reckon you're going to have your work cut out feeding him. He's going to be a real trencher-man.'

'Just like his father, then,' Julie said affectionately.

The couple exchanged a loving glance, and Jo looked away, staring down into her mug and wondering if Ed was all right now. He seemed fine, though, bright and perky, laughing with the Browns and seeming to enjoy himself while the baby tucked into his first proper meal.

Perhaps he really had been feeling queasy? She had driven rather fast.

Jo checked her watch, surprised to find that it was two hours since baby Michael had been born, and packed up her things. 'We'll be on our way now. Don't overdo it.'

'Would I?' Julie said with a smile.

Jo arched a brow, shrugged into her coat and loaded everything into the car with Ed's help.

'Take care, now, and ring me if you're worried. I'll check you again before ten, but call if you want anything.'

'We will, and thanks,' Tim said, and gave her a hug. He shook Ed's hand, and then they were off, bumping down the track towards the road.

'It's got colder,' she said, fiddling with the heater controls, and wished she'd got a pair of gloves. Laura had borrowed them, of course, like she borrowed everything these days. Goodness knows if she'd ever see them again.

They turned onto the main road and headed back towards the surgery. Out of deference to his nerves she drove much more slowly, and Ed commented on it.

'In case you hadn't noticed, we were none too early,' she reminded him with a laugh.

'Yes. I can see why you went fast—did you think she was that far on?'

Jo nodded. 'There was something in her voice—after a while you get an instinct for the little nuances. She just sounded—well, close, I suppose is the best way to describe it.'

'She was certainly that!'

He fell silent, and she drove back into Yoxburgh in the dark with her headlights gleaming on the frosty road. As she pulled up at the surgery she turned to him in the dark car.

'Ed—are you OK?'

He paused, his hand on the doorhandle, and looked at her warily. 'Fine. Why shouldn't I be?'

She shrugged. 'I don't know. I just thought—what happened back there? My driving isn't that bad, so what was it all about?'

He gave a wry smile. 'You noticed. Sometimes...' He

sighed. 'Sometimes I just get a bit choked. I wonder what it would be like—I expect you do the same.'

She relaxed, relieved that there was apparently no great tragedy hanging over him. 'I've got a daughter,' she told him. 'I know all about it—the pluses and the minuses.'

He looked surprised. 'I didn't realise you were married.'

'I'm not. I'm a single parent—always have been,' she added, so he understood her situation.

'Oh. I see. That can't be easy.'

'My mother helps. I couldn't manage without her.'

Her mobile phone rang, and she answered it, then turned to him with a sigh.

'Problems?' he said.

'I have to go out again—one of my mums might be in labour, and she wants to see me. I'll sort the car out, reload my box and go over there. You coming?'

'Do you need me?'

His voice was soft, and something funny happened in her chest—something she didn't understand, something that came out of nowhere and left her feeling empty and confused and a little breathless.

'No—no, I don't need you,' she told him hastily, and wondered if it was true...

CHAPTER TWO

'MUM?'

A door crashed in the distance, and Jo met her mother's eyes with a rueful grin. 'So much for our peaceful teabreak.'

'Mum?' Footsteps retreated, then returned, attached to a bright smile in a pretty heart-shaped face the image of Jo's. Long dark hair, again like her mother's, was scooped up into a band, and now at the end of the day strands escaped, drifting round her soft hazel eyes and giving her a dreamy look.

'Here you are. Hi, Grannie. Wow, a cake! Yum—can I have a bit?' She cut a chunk, hitched herself up onto a stool by the breakfast bar and sank her teeth into the cake, without waiting for a reply—or a plate.

Her grandmother slid a plate under the hovering hand and smiled. 'Good day, darling?'

'OK, I s'pose. Bit pointless at homework club because the staff hadn't got round to giving us any homework yet, but that was cool. We talked about Cara's new boyfriend.' Her eyes swivelled to her mother. 'Talking of which, I hear your new doctor's rather gorgeous.'

Jo nearly choked on her tea. 'I wouldn't have gone that far. He's all right, I suppose.'

'Cara's mum said he was really yummy. So's this cake—can I have another bit?'

'Will you eat your supper?'

Laura rolled her eyes. 'Mother, when do I ever not?'

It was true. She ate like a horse, thank God, in these days of eating disorders and unhappy children with appalling self-images and huge expectations hanging over them. 'OK,' she agreed, and cut a rather more moderate slice. No point in going to the other extreme. 'So, let's hear about Love's Young Dream, then.'

'Cara's boyfriend?' Laura giggled. 'Oh, he's in year nine—the third-year seniors, a year above me, Grannie,' she explained patiently to her far-from-senile grandmother, 'and he's tall and his hair's streaked blond and he's got an earring and a tattoo on his bum.'

'Bottom,' Jo corrected automatically. 'And how does Cara know that?' she added, dreading the answer.

Laura laughed. 'He had to do a moonie for a forfeit at a party she went to—she says it's a dragon and it's really cute.'

'Let's hope no one gets the urge to stick a sword in it,' Jo's mother said pragmatically, and cleared the breakfast bar while Jo tried not to choke.

'Can't I have any more?' Laura said in her best feel-sorry-for-me voice, watching the cake vanish into a tin, but her grandmother was unmoved.

'You'll just be sick. Go and wash your hands and come down for supper in half an hour.'

She disappeared, leaving her coat dropped over a chair and her shoes scattered on the kitchen floor where she'd kicked them off.

'A tattoo, eh?' Rebecca Halliday said with a murmur as the pounding footsteps faded up the stairs.

Jo rolled her eyes and picked up the shoes and the coat, tidying them away. 'Whatever next. I wish I could influence her choice of friends a bit more—she worries me.'

'She's fine. She's a sensible girl. She won't get into trouble.'

'You thought I was sensible,' Jo reminded her pointedly. 'So did I, come to that, and we were both wrong.'

'You *were* sensible. You were lied to. We all were.'

'You're very loyal, Mum.'

Her mother hugged her briefly. 'You've come through.' She dropped her arms and moved away, not given to overt displays of affection, and started scrubbing carrots like a woman possessed.

Jo helped her, and after a moment her mother looked up and met her eyes. 'So, tell me about this doctor, then. Gorgeous, eh?'

Jo could feel the tell-tale colour creeping up her neck, and busied herself with the casserole. 'Oh, he's just a man, Mum. Nothing special.'

'Married?'

Funny how one word could carry so very many little nuances. 'No, he's not married,' Jo said patiently. 'He's thirty-two, single, he started working in hospital obstetrics and decided he wanted to be a GP so he retrained. He's been doing locum for six months while he looked for a job.'

'And now he's ready to settle down.'

Jo put the lid back on the casserole with a little bang. 'How should I know? He's only been working since the first of January, we've had a weekend when he's been off and it's only the fifth now!'

Her mother slid the carrot pan onto the hob and flicked the switch. 'Don't get crabby, I was only asking. Anyway, you usually have them down pat in the first ten minutes.'

'No, that's Sue. I usually take fifteen.'

Rebecca laughed. 'Sorry. I stand corrected.' She deftly changed the subject. 'I gather Julie Brown had her baby yesterday.'

'Yes—another boy. Both well. I was so busy I didn't have time to tell you. It was a lovely delivery—on the kitchen table.'

Her mother smiled. 'So I gather. That'll make meal-times interesting for them. How about a glass of wine?'

'What a good idea.'

Jo took the proffered glass and followed her mother into the sitting room, dropping into the comfy sofa and resting her head back against the high cushion. It was more comfortable than her own little annexe at the other end of the house where she usually spent her time after work, but tonight her mother had cooked for them and obviously felt a little lonely.

So did Jo so that was fine. Since her father had died they'd found companionship and support in each other, and without her, as she'd told Ed, she wouldn't have been able to cope with bringing Laura up and keeping her career—

'It would have been your father's sixtieth birthday to-day,' her mother said quietly into the silence.

Jo's eyes flew open. 'Oh, Mum, I'm sorry, I forgot,' she said, filled with remorse.

'He was going to retire—funny how you make all these plans and the decisions get taken away from you and changed. I can't believe it's nearly four years since he died.'

'Or nearly thirteen since I had Laura. He really adored her.'

'Yes. They were great friends.'

Jo swirled her wine round and peered through it at the lights. 'You must miss him.'

'I do—every day, but life goes on.' She sat quietly for a moment, her teeth worrying the inside of her lip, then she met Jo's eyes. 'Maurice wants me to go to dinner at the weekend. I said I'd think about it.'

Jo thought of Maurice Parker, the senior partner who was due to retire soon and whose place Ed would fill, and wondered what her father would have thought.

They'd been colleagues and friends for years—would he have minded? Would Maurice's wife have minded, after all the suffering she'd gone through before she died? Would she even have known what was going on?

It was as if her mother read her mind. 'He had such a difficult time with Betty—Alzheimer's is such a cruel disease,' she said. 'She didn't know him, you know, not for the last three years. Your father used to say she'd be the death of him.'

'He aged, certainly. He looks much better now in the last couple of years without all the strain of her illness to weigh him down.'

'Awful, what love and loyalty can do to you. Must check the carrots and put the broccoli on.'

Jo let her go, sipped her wine and thought about her father. He'd always seemed so fit until the heart attack that killed him. There'd been no warning, no time to prepare. One minute he'd been there, the next he'd gone. Her mother had been devastated, and Laura too. Jo had been so busy propping them both up she'd hardly had time to grieve, and by the time she'd lifted her head above water again it had seemed too late, a little contrived.

She had grieved, though, in the privacy of her own room, shedding huge, silent tears for the man who'd been so fair and so kind to her all her life.

He'd been her best friend, a rock when Laura had been born, and without his support she wouldn't have been able to train. True, her mother had looked after the baby, but it had been her father who'd encouraged her and supported her financially, bought her a car and paid the running expenses and paid for everything Laura had needed.

They'd turned one end of the house into a separate annexe, giving Jo and her baby privacy but easy access for babysitting, and with their help she'd built herself a career of which she was proud.

Then suddenly, without warning, he'd gone, leaving Maurice, and James Kalbraier, to cope with the practice. Maurice had cut down his hours, taken on another doctor, Mary Brady, and concentrated on nursing Betty for the last few years of her life.

And now Jo's mother was talking about going out to dinner with Maurice.

Jo considered the idea, and decided it was a good one. They'd both loved their spouses, but they were gone and Maurice and Rebecca were still alive.

Yes. It would do them both good to get out. Who knows, they might—

'Supper!'

'Coming!'

She took her wine glass through into the kitchen and put it down by the sink. 'Mmm, smells good. Have you called Laura?'

'Well, I did yell, but she's got that music on so loud...'

'I'll get her,' Jo said with a grin, and ran upstairs. She banged on the door which was vibrating gently with the music her daughter was listening to, and opened it a crack. 'Supper, darling.'

'OK.' The noise vanished, and the silence was deafening.

'You really shouldn't have it on so loud,' she began, but Laura laughed and skipped past her, flitting down the stairs and running through to her grandmother's kitchen, ignoring the predictable lecture.

'Hi, Grannie, what's for supper—? Oh, yum! Can I help?'

Jo smiled and followed her through more slowly. She wasn't a bad kid—just a little loud, with questionable taste in friends. She supposed she could send Laura to the independent school her mother kept offering to pay for, but that would mean travelling to school, no convenient buses and after-school homework clubs, and her friends would be scattered far and wide.

This way, questionable though some of them might be, they were nearby, and when Jo was working that was very important.

'We've got a panto rehearsal tonight,' Laura reminded her as she joined them at the table. 'Will you test me on my lines?'

Jo laughed humourlessly. 'Just so long as you don't try and test me—I haven't had time to look at them since before Christmas.'

'Mother! Roz will skin you alive!'

'Don't I know it! I'll try and have a quick scan through after supper—perhaps Grannie will test you.'

'Of course I will, darling. How's it going?'

Jo laughed. 'It was awful before Christmas. We'll see if anyone has spent the last couple of weeks learning their lines or if they've all switched off and forgotten what little they did know. I suspect the latter.'

'Based on personal experience?' her mother said sagely, and Jo gave a rueful chuckle.

'You guessed. Oh, well, there's time.'

'Have they got anyone else for the chorus yet?' Laura asked, tucking into her casserole with huge enthusiasm.

'I don't know.'

'You ought to ask Dr What's-his-name—what *is* his name? The new guy?'

'Latimer—Ed Latimer. I doubt if he'd be interested.'

'You could ask,' she suggested round a forkful of carrots.

She could—but she didn't want to. She didn't want Ed Latimer any nearer her than he had to be, for any more time than was absolutely necessary. He was too disturbing, too masculine. Too male. Just—too much.

She finished her meal in silence, listening with half an ear to Laura and her mother chattering, then she loaded the dishwasher and excused herself for a quick shower before the rehearsal. The water was warm and silky and sensuous, sliding over her naked skin and making her aware of herself in a way she'd almost forgotten.

Her mind turned to Ed again, and she closed her eyes and moaned softly. Why? She'd spent years fending off flirts, and none of them had even so much as ruffled the surface of her peaceful existence.

And now Ed Latimer had come strolling into her life, his hands shoved casually into his pockets, all testosterone and laughing eyes, and her self-control was lying on the floor, belly-up and grinning like a submissive dog!

'This is awful! What on earth's the matter with all of you? Two weeks off and you've all keeled over and died!'

There was a chorus of feeble protest, and their hard-pressed producer threw down her script and stalked into the kitchen. Jo met Laura's eyes and smiled encouragingly, then went into the kitchen after Roz, closing the door quietly.

'Roz?'

'It's like this every year! I don't know why I do it! They screech through by the skin of their teeth, just about pulling the thing together by the final dress rehearsal—sometimes not even then! This is the thirteenth year, you realise that? I knew we ought to give it a rest, but they wouldn't listen. It'll be fine, they all said, and now look at them! Corpsed, the lot of them, the second you take their scripts away! Well, that's it. They're not having their scripts again, any of them, and they can just manage with the prompt!'

Jo soothed Roz's ruffled feathers and gave her time to settle down. 'Perhaps we ought to have our break early and let everyone calm down a bit—the urn's hot now. Why don't I make a big pot of tea and open the biscuits and we'll try again in a little while?'

Roz stabbed her hands through her hair and gave a stifled scream. 'They drive me nuts,' she confessed.

'You love it.'

'I know. I must be a masochist.'

They shared a smile, and Jo filled the teapot while Roz poured milk into the cups. 'We still need another man for the chorus—I don't suppose your new doctor wants to get involved?' Roz asked her.

She slopped the tea into a saucer and splashed her hand. 'Damn,' she muttered, and put down the pot. 'I don't know—why don't you ask him? I expect he'll be too busy.'

'Would you ask him for me, as you'll see him?'

And, just like that, she was forced into a corner from which there was no escape.

'Hi, there.'

Shivers ran up Jo's spine and made her hair tingle against her scalp. She turned, groping for a smile that wasn't completely idiotic, and forced herself to meet Ed's eyes. 'Hi, there, yourself,' she said, and was very proud of the fact that her voice only croaked the tiniest bit.

'How are things? Any imminent obstetrics for me?'

'Sorry.' She shook her head and smiled a more natural smile. 'They're all hanging on till their due dates.'

'Even your lady the other night?'

'Even her. Sorry. I've got an antenatal class at the

hospital in a minute—I'll ask them if they want to get a wriggle on for you, shall I?'

He chuckled and reached out to test the kettle, and the sun slanting through the window caught his hair, gleaming on the red lights in it and turning it a rich, deep chestnut. It was a lovely colour, much more interesting than plain dark brown, and she wanted to reach out and touch it...

'There should be enough in there for you,' she told him, dragging her attention back to the kettle. 'It's just boiled.'

'Tea for you?'

'I'm OK.' She held up her full mug to show him, and he nodded and snagged a mug off the draining-board.

'No doubt they'll all produce in the fullness of time,' he said, going back to their previous conversation. 'We've had two in the past week—I suppose that's my ration.'

'Absolutely. I've got something to ask you, by the way, talking of producing. The thirteenth annual Yoxburgh panto is short of a male chorus member—Roz asked me to ask you, but I told her you'd be too busy.'

He turned and met her eyes. 'Why?'

'Why are they short?'

'Why did you tell her I'd be too busy?'

She felt a little touch of colour brush her cheeks. 'I don't know—I just thought you would be,' she faltered. 'It's quite a punishing rehearsal schedule. It's up to you. Of course, if you want to do it you'd be more than welcome—I was just trying to give you a way out if you wanted one. It can be pretty tedious.'

She floundered to a halt and looked up at him again, to find him watching her with understanding.

'If you don't want me to do it, just say so, Jo,' he

murmured, and his voice was like raw silk, sliding over her nerve endings.

She laughed, a forced little hiccup of sound. 'Don't be daft. I just thought you wouldn't be interested. It's very amateur.'

'Are you in it?'

She nodded. 'Yes—for my sins, I've got the female lead. Heaven knows when I'll get time to learn the lines.'

'Is it fun?' he asked, and with a sudden flash of insight she realised he was lonely and would actually like to join in. Good grief, a willing volunteer. That was a first!

It was beyond her to exclude him just for her own selfish reasons.

'Yes, it is fun,' she told him, relenting. 'It would help your patients get to know you as a person as well. It could be good for your image—they're a bit slow to let you in round here.'

He shot her a quizzical look. 'I noticed.'

She coloured again, and looked down at her hands. 'I'm sorry. I just felt that if we had to work together all the time and ended up at the panto rehearsals, well, it might be a bit...'

'Much?'

She nodded.

'Does it unsettle you?' he asked softly. 'My proximity?'

She looked up into his eyes—those stunningly magnetic storm-grey eyes that seemed to see right to the heart of her—and nodded again, just slightly. 'A little,' she confessed.

His mouth tipped in a crooked and endearing grin. 'That makes two of us. I'm not exactly immune to you, either.'

She stood up, pushing her chair back and trying for a bit of authority. 'That doesn't mean we have to do anything about it. We have to work together, Ed. I don't think we can do that if we're...' She ran out of words, unusually for her, but he was there again.

'Involved?' he offered. A lazy smile lurked in his eyes.

'Exactly.'

He shrugged and grinned again. 'OK. If I promise to keep my distance, can I join the pantomime?'

'Of course you can.' She returned his smile. 'It is awful, though. Don't say you haven't been warned.'

He chuckled. 'OK. When's the next rehearsal?'

'Tonight. Quarter to eight, at the community hall. Wear something warm—it can be a bit chilly.'

He nodded, drained his tea and left her. She sat again, as if she were a puppet whose strings had been cut, and buried her face in her hands. So he felt it too—and she'd thought it was just her, being silly. Oh, Lord, this was so much more complicated. If she was the only one—

'You OK?'

Her head jerked up. 'Yes, just a bit tired. Did you forget something?'

'Where's the community hall?' Ed asked.

'Ah. Um—on the main street, nearly opposite the chip shop.'

'That black and white building?'

She nodded, avoiding those searching eyes. 'That's right.'

'OK. I'll see you then—unless you're back in the surgery after your antenatal class?'

'Antenatal class?' She gasped and leapt to her feet. 'I'd forgotten it!' she muttered, and, scooping up her pager from the table, she headed for the door.

'See you later,' he called. Jo ran out to her car, wondering if she'd been totally insane to suggest he should join the pantomime crew. Her brains were scrambled enough as it was!

She arrived at the hospital just about on time, and a couple of the mums were late. She decided to give them a minute or two because they were new. While they waited she ticked the names of those who were there on her register and encouraged them to mix and get to know each other while she set up her equipment.

She had a doll and a plastic pelvis so that they could see the way the baby would emerge through the birth canal, charts and diagrams to show the development of the baby, and lots of information about nutrition, exercise and so on.

The classes didn't have a beginning or an end, but ran on a continuous loop, with four sessions making up the whole set. In a way it made it harder, but it did mean that someone new to the area or only able to come intermittently didn't miss out. Each session included a lecture, a discussion and work on relaxation and pain control, and today was about the second stage of labour, the expulsive stage.

The latecomers arrived together, apologising for getting lost on the way, and Jo called all the patients to order, settled them down and started the class, by going round and asking the new members in turn to say a little about themselves, whether it was their first or subsequent child and what sort of delivery they were hoping for.

There were five women out of the ten there who wanted a home birth or who wanted to deliver in the GP unit. Of these five, only three were on Jo's mental list of possibles. One was a little too old, another had a previous history of stillbirth.

The other three couldn't deliver in the GP unit on the grounds that only second and third babies were permitted by their scheme, and these were all first-timers. Still, they could, if she thought they were suitable, opt for a home birth with consultant back-up, if necessary, at Jo's discretion. She still hadn't decided.

The older mother, however, was aware that Jo didn't want her to deliver at home, but it didn't stop her planning a home delivery, and Jo knew full well that when it came to the crunch she'd leave it too late to go to hospital, regardless of what they might say to convince her otherwise.

'I'd like to have the baby in the GP unit,' one of the new mums was saying, 'but I know I can't because it's my first, and my husband isn't happy about me having it at home. I'd like to come back to the GP unit straight afterwards, though.'

Jo nodded. 'That should be possible if everything goes well, or if you have support at home afterwards you wouldn't need to come in here at all.'

She looked doubtful. 'I don't know if I could cope alone. It's such a responsibility—what happens if you don't know why it's crying?'

Some of the others chorused their agreement, and Jo hastened to reassure them. 'You struggle on and try everything until you hit on something that works. Babies are remarkably tough and very good at getting their own way—I really wouldn't worry.'

'But what if I'm really clueless?' she persisted.

'You'll know what to do. I've only had one mum in all my years who genuinely didn't, and she gradually relaxed and started listening to the baby. You'll be fine—and, anyway, you wouldn't be alone. For the first ten days I'll come whenever you want, and once a day in any case, then the health visitor takes over so you won't be abandoned.'

She looked round. 'Right. A couple of you are second- or third-timers along for a refresher and the rest of you

are having your first so I think we'll have input and
comments from the old hands after the talk. I want to
go through labour and delivery with you, just to make
sure you all know or remember what all the stages are
and what's happening at any point.'

They settled down and listened, and after Jo had done
her demonstration with the elastic band and the plastic
pelvis she invited questions and comments.

This was always a tricky one. Inevitably there would
be at least one mother who would revel in going over
the more traumatic and memorable moments of her labour, regardless of the dread she was inspiring in the
first-time mums, so Jo was on the alert ready to cut off
anyone who launched into a counter-productive
monologue.

In fact, they were fine, and after a few minutes she
got them all to lie down and relax.

'Think of every part of your body in turn. As you
think of it, tense it hard, then hold it, then let it flop.
Think about how you make it go floppy, and after a
while you'll be able to home in on tight areas of your
body and relax them. Right, start with your feet. Point
your toes hard, but make sure you don't get cramp.
Good. Hold—and relax. Totally floppy. Good. Now pull
your feet up so your toes are pointing at your head.
Tense—hold—and flop. Well done.'

She watched them, looking for the ones who found it
difficult and the ones who had probably done yoga or
had been to her classes before.

One new girl, thin and dressed in what Jo could only
describe as 'hippy' clothes, was wonderfully relaxed.
Her name was Mel, and Jo flicked through her notes and
noticed her address—the travellers' site in the forest outside Yoxburgh, up on the heath by the edge of the trees.

It was a lovely spot, but Jo had a sneaky feeling, despite what she'd said, that Mel was going to go for a home delivery. The idea of delivering a baby in a converted coach or, worse still, a 'bender'—a shelter made of tree branches—filled Jo with horror.

What if anything went wrong? It was Mel's first— there was no reason why anything should go wrong, but what if it did? The baby was bound to be born at night— the more difficult the location the more likely it seemed to be, and there was no power out there, no light, no running water. How would she deliver her safely under those conditions? Jo vowed to have a word to make sure Mel understood the risks. Mel had a few weeks left to go so she'd use them to try and talk sense into her.

Jo led them through the relaxation, then the breathing, and finally she got them to grip each other's forearms with both hands and twist firmly in opposite directions to pull the skin. Called 'Chinese burns', they were a thing schoolchildren did to each other to see who was bravest—harmless but painful, Jo found they were a useful tool to help women practise breathing through the 'contractions' and remaining relaxed. When they'd all had a rest for a moment and she'd done the question-and-answer session and they'd put the mats away, she sent them all off.

Still thinking about Mel, she packed up all her stuff, cleared away the cups and made sure the mats had all been stacked properly in the cupboard. They used the maternity day-room for their classes, and she didn't want to leave the place untidy.

One of the staff midwives stuck her head round the door and grinned. 'Got time for a cuppa?'

'I'd love one. Did you see my traveller?'

'Yes—is she going to be a problem?'

Jo laughed. 'I hope not, but I suspect so. I think she's just unconventional, not stupid, but I've got a suspicion

I won't be able to persuade her to go to the Audley. I just have a feeling.'

'Birth in a bender, eh? That'll be a first, won't it?'

'Don't.' Jo sipped her tea and sighed with relief. 'Perhaps I'll get Ed Latimer to talk to her—see what he's made of.'

'I don't know, but if you can get the recipe, I'd like one the same, please!'

Jo laughed, but inside her stomach the butterflies were working themselves up to a frenzy. The remark had reminded her about Ed, and about the rehearsal. It was panto time in three hours, and she'd have no professional guise to hide behind, no protocol—just herself, and Laura.

That was it! She'd be Laura's mother. It would make her seem middle-aged and boring—with any luck!

CHAPTER THREE

ED PAUSED outside the black and white mock-timbered building that was the Yoxburgh and District Community Hall, and wondered if he was out of his mind.

Jo had made it pretty clear that she found his presence disturbing, and that the sensation wasn't welcome. In a way he felt the same, and yet there was something about her that drew him so forcefully that he just didn't seem to be able to ignore it.

He didn't want to be a nuisance, and he was being very careful not to crowd her at work or flirt with her, but every cell in his body was screaming for more contact—and the pantomime seemed like a gift from the gods.

Anyway, Jo aside, he had to get to know people and make some friends. He couldn't be GP to all of them— surely there'd be lots of people who'd be happy to be social without fear of compromising their relationship.

His father was a country GP and they'd always had a fairly hectic social life, but Jo had warned him about the locals, not letting newcomers in.

Well, he'd find out, wouldn't he? He put his hand against the door and pushed, and found himself sucked into a fantasy world. Little bees ran about the floor, giggling and shrieking, a young girl was complaining that her dragon didn't do up down the back and could the hooks be moved, costumes were piled in heaps on every surface, and in the middle of it all stood Jo in a wedding dress, her hair pinned up and a tiara perched in the dark, gleaming curls, laughing with a tall man in a blue satin suit with floppy lace cuffs.

He bent and said something and Jo laughed, her eyes sparkling at the joke they shared—and Ed wanted to kill him.

She turned just as the murderous thought was being put aside, and he wasn't sure if he imagined it or if a flicker of panic brushed her eyes. Then she excused herself and came over to him, weaving her way through the crowd.

'I thought you'd bottled out—you're late.'

'I couldn't get away from the surgery—someone collapsed in the waiting room with a tummy bug and I admitted her to the hospital for fluids and supervision. It took ages. Anyway, I'm here now. Who do I need to see?'

'Roz—she's going through a scene. Come with me.'

He followed her, wondering how she could look so radiantly beautiful in what on close inspection seemed to be a set of net curtains skilfully flung together into a wedding dress. 'Roz, this is Ed Latimer,' Jo was saying, and he smiled automatically and shook her hand.

'Oh, you look very useful,' Roz was saying, eyeing him up with a grin. 'Can you sing?'

He chuckled. 'Well enough, I expect. Why?'

'Because the other male chorus can't. Go and see Anne for a costume, and we'll get you kitted up as a villager to start with. It might be tricky—you're quite big, aren't you? Then you need to see Mr Music over there—Andrew, we've got a new victim for the chorus. Can you give him a music sheet? Here's a script—you're a love. Thanks.'

And Roz vanished into a crowd of villagers and the back end of the pantomime horse, leaving him with Jo.

He looked down at the script. '*Beauty and the Beast*, eh?'

'Yes.'

'And you're the Beauty?'

She nodded. 'Belle.'

'How appropriate,' he murmured, and she tutted and gave him a look. 'You want me to lie?' he asked, but it didn't help. She sighed and stepped away from him, looking back over her shoulder.

'Come on, I'll take you to Anne,' she said shortly, and he reminded himself he'd promised to keep his distance. Damn. Why couldn't he keep his mouth shut?

They were crossing the room towards the back when a girl of about twelve skidded up to them and slithered to a halt. 'Hi—I'm Laura. Are you the new GP?'

He eyed her with interest. She was unmistakably Jo's daughter, from the tip of her pert little nose to the soles of her stocking-clad feet, and she was eyeing him very, very frankly.

'Yes, I am,' he replied, wondering why she was so interested.

'This is my mum,' she told him unnecessarily.

'I guessed. Pleased to meet you, Laura.'

'So, are you going to be in the panto?' she asked, her head on one side in a gesture so reminiscent of her mother it was almost comical.

'Looks like it,' he told her.

'Good—Mum thought you wouldn't want to, but I think you'll like it. It's a laugh.'

'Laura! They need you for song practice!' Jo said.

'Oops—have to fly. See you.'

She shot off across the room to the man at the keyboard, and without any further incident Ed was introduced to Anne, measured and sized up and offered an armful of musty clothes to try at home later.

Breeches, a full-sleeved white shirt, a waistcoat, long socks—he was going to look a peach! Ah, well, it was all in a good cause...

Jo tried to concentrate, but every time she looked across at Ed the air seemed to crackle between them and she forgot her lines.

Predictably Roz got cross and scolded her, and she got through the rest of the rehearsal by not looking at him. Blow Roz and her invitation! It would have been so much easier if he hadn't been there—and much less fun, she had to admit as they were practising the winter medley.

Ed had a lovely voice, deep and rich and full, and he was instantly seconded to sing a solo for the Beast, who had no voice at all. As the Beast would have a huge mask on at the time, it didn't matter that the voice would come from behind the scenes.

He was taken off to practise it, and Laura came up to Jo and tugged her sleeve. 'He's gorgeous! I think you should marry him,' she whispered.

Jo coloured and shushed her daughter. 'Laura, don't be silly. I hardly know him,' she whispered back.

'So get to know him.'

'No—look, I'm not talking about this here. Just hush.'

The rehearsal was wrapped up at about ten, and Jo scooped up her costumes and rounded up Laura. Ed was standing by the door chatting to a group of men, and they were stopped on the way out by the groom, the back end of the horse and the Beast. 'We're going up to the Dog and Fox—want to join us? Ed's coming.'

She met his eyes, reading nothing from them for a change, and shook her head. 'No—I'd love to but I mustn't. I'm on call tomorrow night, and this young lady's got school tomorrow. Perhaps another time.'

Was that a flicker of disappointment, or relief?

Hard to tell—his face hadn't really moved a muscle. They snuggled down into their coats for the short walk back to the house, and as they cut through the little side streets Laura was clearly fizzling.

'What is it?' Jo asked her, resigned to a lecture.

'Him—Ed Latimer. I just think he's perfect for you.'

Jo sighed. 'He's just a man, Laura!'

'So—what do you want, a woman?'

'Of course not—'

'So stop saying he's just a man. It's the right starting point, at least! And, anyway, he's not just a man, he's gorgeous, and he's a doctor, so you've got medicine in common, and he's the right age—I can't see the problem!'

No. At the age of twelve, Jo doubted if she would have seen the problem, either. It was only as she'd grown older and wiser that the pitfalls had become obvious.

Like the fact, for example, that he was thirty-two and still single.

There had to be a reason for that. Most men of that age were married, divorced, living with someone in a settled relationship or just not fit to live with. She knew he wasn't married or divorced, she knew he was living with Dr Parker for now until he found somewhere, and there didn't seem to be a woman on the scene. That left unfit to live with.

Wow! What an option!

Something else was worrying her, too. She slung an arm around Laura and gave her a little hug. 'Why are you trying to marry me off, anyway?' she asked lightly. 'Aren't we OK as we are?'

Laura's steps hesitated slightly. 'I suppose—it's just that sometimes you look sort of lonely, and there are things we can't manage to do—lifting things and stuff like that. It would be useful to have a man around some-times.'

Jo chuckled and hugged Laura hard. 'Darling, I can't just marry someone because it would be useful to have a man around to lift things!'

'No, I s'pose not. Still, if he was the right man...'

'He's not,' she said emphatically, and changed the subject fast.

'Ah, Jo—could we have a word?'

She paused in the corridor. 'Sure. What can I do for you, Dr Parker?'

'Um—I wondered if you're busy on Saturday night?'

'Me?' She looked up into Maurice Parker's kindly eyes and wondered what he was up to. 'No, not that I'm aware of. Why?'

'Because I've invited your mother round for dinner, and Ed will be there, of course, as he's staying with me, and—ah—well, I thought if there were some other peo-ple there too—well, it might make it a little less, well, intimate, really,' he concluded, and his neck went an interesting shade of brick.

Realisation dawned. After all the years of his marriage to Betty, Maurice Parker was shy about dating her mother—and her mother was probably shy about dating him.

How lovely.

She smiled, suppressing the little flutter of nerves be-cause she was going to be spending the evening with Ed as well, coincidentally, and agreed without hesitation. 'That would be lovely, Dr Parker. Thank you, I'll look forward to it. What time would you like us?'

'Eight?'

'Right. How formal are we being?'

He laughed. 'Well, I can't cook for nuts so don't dress

up too much or you'll put me to shame. I tell you what, let's call it supper, shall we?'

She shared a smile. 'Let's. We'll see you at eight.'

And I get to spend the evening with Ed, she thought again, and wondered how she'd cope.

Not that she could have got out of it, of course. There was no way she could let Maurice down, and dating again after all that time must be awful.

She tried to imagine how she'd feel, hardly having dated at all since before Laura's birth, and a shiver of nervous anticipation ran through her veins. She'd been out, of course, but mainly with people from work or the pantomime, and always in a group.

She hadn't been out alone with a man since Laura had appeared on the scene, and the very thought made her mouth dry and her heart pound. How would it feel, to be alone with Ed, for instance? What would he do? Would he try and kiss her goodnight?

And would she let him?

She thought about the firm, chiselled lips that were so ready to quirk into a smile, and wondered how they'd feel against her own.

A tiny moan escaped her, and her eyes fluttered shut. Exquisite—

'Jo?'

Her eyes flew open, hot colour flooding her cheeks, and with a muttered excuse she pushed past Ed and went into the kitchen.

He followed her, letting the door close behind them, and she could feel his eyes on her. 'Are you all right?'

'Fine—just a bit hot,' she told him, and wished she had a better grip on her emotions. She didn't want to react to him—she wanted to be professional and impartial and neutral—

No, she didn't. She wanted to be kissed until her

bones melted and her lungs were bursting and her heart sang.

'Idiot,' she muttered.

'What?'

'Nothing. I've forgotten to order something,' she lied. 'Did you want to see me, Dr Latimer?'

'Ed—and, no, not really. You looked a little shocked in the corridor. I wondered if everything was all right.'

'Fine,' she said in what she hoped was a breezy voice, and flashed him a brilliant smile. 'I gather we're both going to be playing gooseberry on Saturday night so my mother and Maurice Parker don't feel too threatened by their date.'

He looked surprised. 'Is it a date?'

'I think so. Sounds like it.'

His mouth softened into a smile. 'How delightful. I shall look forward to gooseberrying with you—it'll make a change from learning the panto songs.' And he clicked his heels together, tipped his head in a little bow and left her.

'I feel as if I'm sixteen again,' Rebecca said crossly. 'It's ridiculous, at my age!' She stood back from the mirror and patted her stomach, frowning at the little bulge which was all but hidden by the flowing lines of her dress. 'I'm getting fat—are you sure this dress looks all right?'

Jo sighed. 'Mum, you look wonderful. Stop worrying. Maurice Parker didn't invite you for dinner so he could measure your waist!'

'Why *did* he invite me?' she asked softly, sitting on the end of the bed beside her daughter.

'Because he likes you? Because he respects you, and cares about you? Maybe even because he finds you attractive?'

Rebecca blushed. 'Don't be silly! I'm nearly sixty!'

'So's he. What's wrong with that?'

'Well—nothing, I suppose. If he was thirty I'd have something to worry about.'

'Exactly. Now, are you ready?'

Rebecca ran a critical eye over her daughter. 'I am, but I don't think you are. What are you wearing?'

Jo blinked. 'Well—this.'

'No. Go and put something pretty on, not that plain dress that makes you look like a secretary.'

'It's the only suitable thing I've got—unless you want me to wear the trousers I use for work?'

Her mother tutted and stood, going to her wardrobe and rummaging through the rails of clothes. 'What about this? Your father always used to say I looked wonderful in it, and we're about the same size except for the tummy.'

'You haven't got a tummy.'

'Nor have you, so it should be fine. Try it.'

Jo took the dress her mother thrust at her, holding it up against her. It was a lovely muted charcoal blue, almost navy, a softly draping knitted dress with long sleeves. It came down almost to her ankles, and had a wonderfully flattering deep cowl neck.

'It'll look lovely with those navy boots of yours. Put it on, and it needs a belt—here.'

Jo shrugged, unzipped the formal dress she was wearing and slipped the new one over her head, then belted it with the broad navy leather belt her mother handed her.

'Much better,' her mother said approvingly. 'Oh, yes, darling, you look fabulous in it! Have it. I'll never wear it again—not now, without your father, and it seems a shame to have it hanging in the cupboard when it looks so pretty on you.' Her mother's eyes filled, and Jo hugged her.

'Are you sure? It was Dad's favourite.'

'He'd approve,' she said firmly. 'Now, get the boots, let your hair down, brush it out and let's go.'

There wasn't time to argue and, anyway, it was her mother's evening out, not hers. She pulled on her big thick coat with the snuggly collar, and they walked the two hundred yards down the road to Maurice's house. The wind was blowing off the sea, but they were used to it and Jo loved it.

She couldn't imagine living anywhere else, and she took a great deep breath of salty air and sighed with contentment. 'What a lovely night—I expect we'll have a frost. The moon's up.'

'Mmm, I expect it'll get my camellia—it does without fail. Do you think Laura will be all right with Cara?'

'Yes—her mother's pretty firm. They'll be watching videos half the night, I expect.'

'She'll be ghastly tomorrow.'

Jo laughed. 'Of course—that's half the fun of a sleep-over. Still, at least she's got a day to get over it. I wonder what's for supper? I'm starving.'

They walked up the path of Maurice Parker's big Victorian seafront house and rang the bell. He opened the door almost instantly, ushering them in and taking their coats, and Jo thought he seemed a little flustered.

He smiled distractedly at Jo, then bent and kissed her mother on the cheek. 'You look enchanting, my dear. It's lovely to see you again.'

Jo felt a lump in her throat. He really did seem genuinely fond of her mother, and it was wonderful to see the smile blossom on her face.

'You don't look so bad yourself these days,' Rebecca

was saying, and patted him on the cheek affectionately. 'It's been a long time, Maurice.'

'Too long,' he murmured, and then seemed to collect himself before leading them into the drawing room. A fire crackled cheerfully in the grate, and Ed unfolded himself from one of the chairs and smiled a greeting.

Maurice cupped her mother's elbow and led her forward, and Jo noticed he seemed nervous. How diverting. He'd never looked even slightly flustered in all the time she'd known him until tonight. She suppressed a smile.

'Rebecca, I'd like you to meet my young lodger, Ed Latimer,' he was saying. 'Ed, this is Rebecca Halliday—and Jo, of course, you know.'

Ed took Rebecca's hand. 'Delighted to meet you, Mrs Halliday.'

'And you—you're the talk of the town. I've heard a lot about you.'

'Not from me,' Jo put in hastily, and Ed laughed.

'I didn't think so for a moment.' He released her mother's hand and turned to Jo. His eyes skimmed over her and came back to her face, approval clear in his eyes. 'You look lovely,' he said softly. 'That colour suits you.'

'Doesn't it?' her mother chipped in. 'She ought to wear things like that more often, but she never goes out.'

'What a waste.'

'I'm busy,' Jo said firmly, and, taking the glass of sherry Maurice held out to her, she retreated to the corner of the settee.

'Fancy a nibble?' Ed asked, settling himself into the settee beside her and leaning towards her with a bowl of peanuts. A teasing smile played around his lips and—whether it was the warmth of the fire, or their bracing walk along the seafront, or just plain Ed, leaning over her with that laughing look in his eyes—she felt her cheeks heating.

'Are you going to behave?' she murmured under her breath, and he laughed and leaned back.

'I only offered you a peanut,' he said softly.

'Really?'

She took a few, nibbling them and trying to ignore his proximity. The rat, he knew he stirred her up!

'So, how's the pantomime going?' Maurice asked her, breaking the silence.

'Oh, well, chaotic as ever. Ed's been sucked in.'

'So I gather—he seems to have enjoyed it. Good way to break into the community. They can be a bit closed at first to strangers, but I suppose that's true of any rural community.'

'Forget rural,' Ed said drily. 'I worked in a city and it was just the same. If you weren't born there, they didn't trust you.'

'I was born here,' Jo told him. 'In a little house just down the road, backing onto ours. We've got it as a holiday cottage now and we let it out, but I can remember growing up there for the first few years until we moved. I was just saying to Mum, I can't imagine living anywhere else now but Yoxburgh.'

'Talking of letting things,' Maurice chipped in, 'Ed's looking for a place to rent—there isn't anything suitable on the market at the moment and he seems to have some fool idea about buying something decrepit and doing it up in his spare time.'

'I just need to wait for the right thing to come on the market, but in the meantime I need a house—I'm driving Maurice crazy being permanently underfoot.'

'How about the cottage?' Rebecca suggested, and Jo felt a flutter of panic. It was too close to their house, much too close!

'Isn't it let?' she said hastily, hoping her mother would pick up her hint, but, no, she ignored it.

'Not till Easter,' she said cheerfully. 'Would that give you long enough? It's sitting idle at the moment, and it would probably do it good to have a tenant. I imagine you're house-trained?'

'Marginally.'

Maurice laughed. 'Oh, he's marvellous. He can cook, too. I confess he's done the meal tonight, but I didn't think a set of TV dinners would impress you.'

Rebecca chuckled, and Jo turned to Ed and arched a brow. 'You cooked? Are we safe?'

'Oh, I should think so. I dropped the meat on the kitchen floor a couple of times, but I gave it a wipe.'

'Right.'

His eyes twinkled, and she let a slow smile touch her lips. 'What are we having?'

'Baked peppers as a starter, *porc aux pruneaux* for the main course and cheese and a fruit fool for pud.'

She blinked in surprise. 'Amazing. Hidden talents.'

'Oh, I've got all sorts of hidden talents,' he murmured, and she felt the embarrassing colour climb her cheeks again.

'Warm in here, isn't it?' he added softly. 'I have to put the veg on—want to give me a hand?'

'Can't you cope?'

'Sure—I just get lonely.'

'Shame,' she teased, but she went with him anyway, carried by legs with a mind of their own. The kitchen was a scene of organised chaos, and she tidied some of the pans away into the sink to soak.

'Leave that. I wanted to talk to you about Maurice and your mother. They seem to be getting on well,' Ed said quietly.

'They always did,' she said, remembering the times they'd all been gathered in this kitchen before Betty's illness and her father's death. 'The four of them were great friends. I've wondered if they'll get together, but they didn't seem to show any sign of it.'

'Giving themselves time?' he suggested. 'I think after something so traumatic you need time to rebuild yourself as a single person. If you've been half of a couple for years and years, it's a hell of a shock.'

'He's sweet with her.'

'He's a gentleman. She'll be safe, Jo. He won't hurt her.'

'I didn't imagine he would,' she replied, then took a deep breath. How odd, to think about her mother in a relationship with anyone but her father. 'Can I do something?' she asked.

'No. Just keep me company. It's nearly done.'

She propped up the worktop and watched him scald the broccoli, mash the potatoes with a huge dollop of *crème fraîche* and put it back into the oven to keep hot, next to the pork steaks.

Then he drained the sprouting broccoli and turned to her with a grin. 'OK, we're done. Shall we get them?'

'That was wonderful!' Rebecca said, setting down her spoon with a sigh. 'Ed, you're very clever.'

'Superb. Excellent meal, thank you,' Maurice added. 'Far better than anything I could have produced.'

'Or me,' Jo said with a laugh. 'I'm spoiled—I've never really had to cook.'

'Ah, well, you have my mother to thank. She gave me a cookery book when I left home, and to my amazement I discovered I enjoyed it—well, this sort of cooking, anyway. Weekday meals are a bit of a drag.'

'You don't say,' Rebecca said with a chuckle. 'You wait till you're sixty and still trying to think up something different!'

'I'll put the coffee on—I can do that,' Maurice offered. 'Ed, why don't you take the girls through to the drawing room—I'll clear this lot.'

'No—we'll clear up. You take Jo,' Rebecca said, and got to her feet and started gathering plates.

Thus dismissed, Jo and Ed went through to the drawing room. Jo sank onto the settee, far too full and very grateful for the expandable nature of the dress, and rested her head against the back cushions.

'That really was a super meal, Ed, thanks,' she said.

She felt the settee dip beside her. 'You're welcome,' he murmured. 'I thought I ought to rescue you—Maurice isn't joking about his cooking.'

She chuckled. 'Oh, dear—that bad, is it?'

'Absolutely. He's a dear, but he can't boil water. I hate to think what the coffee will be like.'

'My mother will help him,' she said lazily from the depths of the cushions. 'It'll be fine.'

'Good.' There was a pause, then she felt him shift in his seat. 'Jo, about this cottage—is it really empty?'

She opened her eyes, wondering if she could put him off, but her generous nature got the better of her. 'Yes— as Mum said, the next let is at Easter.'

'Is it furnished?'

'Oh, yes—fully equipped. It's a holiday cottage, it's got everything.'

'I don't suppose I could look at it?'

'Sure,' she agreed, giving in to the inevitable. 'When?'

He shrugged. 'Whenever—tomorrow?'

'OK.' She glanced at her watch, looking for a diversion. 'I wonder how they're doing? Do you think we ought to go and give them a hand?'

A deep, masculine laugh rippled down the hall towards them, and Ed shook his head. 'I think they sound just fine.'

Pity. She felt altogether too alone with Ed, but it wasn't for many seconds. The others arrived moments later, Maurice bearing a tray of steaming coffee and Rebecca armed with mint thins. They sat on the settee opposite, poured the coffee out and handed round the chocolates, then turned back to each other, totally absorbed.

Jo sipped her coffee and watched them, and she would have had to have been blind not to see the rapport between them. Maurice said something and her mother blushed and dimpled, and beside her Jo could feel Ed chuckle.

She turned her head and met his eyes, and he jerked his head towards the door, one brow arched in enquiry.

She nodded, and they rose and left the room, without the other two even noticing they were gone. Ed pushed the door to and grinned. 'Walk by the sea?' he suggested.

She nodded. 'Good idea. Blow the cobwebs away and work off some of that wonderful food.'

He took Jo's coat off the hook, holding it out for her and snuggling it round her shoulders as she settled into it. Then he shrugged into his own thick quilted jacket, opened the door and ushered her out into the moonlight.

They walked down the path to the sea wall, and the wind tugged at them, reminding them that it was only January.

'Where shall we go?' he asked. They were facing the sea, and she shrugged.

'Want to see the cottage?'

'What, now?'

'Why not?'

'OK.'

They strolled side by side along the sea wall, listening to the crash of the waves on the shingle, and far out to sea they could make out the lights of ships like tiny glow-worms on the horizon. The noise of the town was drowned out by the rush of the sea and the bluster of the wind, and they could have been alone in the world.

It was wonderfully romantic, even though the wind was cold, and she felt herself moving closer to Ed. He stopped, looking out across the sparkling water towards the ships in the distance, and then he turned to her. 'Are you warm enough?'

'Fine—you make a good windbreak,' she said with a smile.

He moved closer. A strand of hair had blown across her face and caught in her mouth, and he lifted a blunt fingertip and brushed it away. His knuckles grazed her cheek, and then his thumb caught on her lip and dragged the soft skin tenderly.

Her lips parted, her eyes searching his in the half-darkness and seeing nothing. She lifted a hand and touched his face, forgetting the distance they were supposed to be keeping—forgetting everything but the man standing between her and the wind. His jaw was rough, the stubble scratchy against her palm. The texture fascinated her.

'Jo?' he murmured. His hands cupped her cold cheeks, and they were warm and firm and gentle. His thumbs grazed her cheekbones, and then he lowered his head and those firm, chiselled lips of her fantasy settled against her mouth like the kiss of an angel.

Sensation exploded in her, making her weak with longing, but it didn't matter. He had hold of her and she wasn't going anywhere. She found her arms under his coat, wrapped around his waist so that her hands were snuggled against the warmth of his back, and his arms enfolded her, supporting her against the broad expanse of his chest while his lips teased and tormented her.

She felt the velvet sweep of his tongue and her lips parted for him. With a ragged groan he cupped her head in one hand to steady her.

The kiss grew deeper, hotter, more urgent, until with a ragged groan he broke it and tucked her head in the hollow under his chin. Her ear was against his throat, and she could hear the thundering of his heart and the uneven rasp of his breath.

'Are you OK?' he murmured after an age.

'I think so. I don't know. Maybe.'

He gave a gruff chuckle and eased away from her. 'Can you stand up?'

'I don't know—can you?'

'Maybe.'

They laughed together, and he reached for her hand, enfolding it in his and leading her back down to the road. 'This cottage,' he said after a moment.

'Hmm?'

'Does it have a bed?'

She stopped dead. 'Yes,' she said warily.

'In which case, I think it might be a very good idea if your mother showed it to me tomorrow, don't you? Because just now, after kissing you like that, I really don't think it would be too smart to be alone with you in a private place—unless you want to?'

She did, possibly more than she'd ever wanted anything, but she knew it was just the knee-jerk reaction of a healthy woman who'd been on her own too long.

'No,' she managed to say, despite the howls of protest from her body. 'In fact, I think I might go home. We're almost there. Do you suppose Maurice will mind walking Mum home?'

'I don't suppose so. It's a beautiful evening.'

She stopped at the front door of their house and turned to him.

'Thank you for the walk—and the meal.'
'My pleasure. We must do it again.'
Do what? she wanted to ask. The walk? The meal?
The kiss…?

CHAPTER FOUR

'DARLING, I hate to be a nuisance but I'm expecting a phone call—you couldn't pop over to the cottage with Ed, could you?'

Rebecca dangled the key in front of Jo and, with him standing there watching, there was no choice. He wondered if Rebecca was on his side, and decided it was quite possible. In fact, he wondered if she'd engineered her daughter's invitation the night before.

Jo took the key. 'Sure. We'll have to go in the back way.'

She led him down the garden, across the narrow alleyway at the back and through the gate into the other garden. Ed looked round at the evergreen plants making a show of colour even then, in January. There was a little porch at the back, with honeysuckle growing over it, and in the summer he imagined it would smell wonderful.

'It's pretty,' he said, studying it as they walked up the path.

'It's just a little Georgian artisan's cottage—nothing special. It's quite sweet, though.' She opened the door in the porch and went in, crossing to the window at the front to pull back the curtains. The winter light flooded in, revealing the clean, simple lines of the furniture and the delicate summery colours.

'It's a little bit musty, I'm afraid, but it's been closed up since October, except for Christmas.'

'It's fine.' Ed looked round the simply furnished sitting room and imagined it with his things there—the hi-fi system, the books, the general clutter that would make it his home—and he felt a smile tug at his lips. 'I like it.'

'You haven't seen the rest—it's not huge,' Jo cautioned.

'There's only me—how huge does it need to be?'

'Oh, well, there's plenty of room for one. We lived here when I was tiny—we used to look over the fence at the one we're in now and say, "That's a nice house. It would be wonderful to live there."'

She laughed. 'Of course we couldn't afford it then, but it came on the market later and we just had to buy it. Then by coincidence a few years later this came up for sale again. My father thought it would be ideal for a holiday cottage, and it's done quite well, really. People seem to like it, anyway.'

'I'm not surprised.'

She was rabbiting, he thought, running on as if she had to fill the silence. Was she so uneasy with him? Perhaps it was because of his remark about the bed last night.

Oh, hell. Surely she realised he wasn't about to jump her bones? 'This is the kitchen,' she said unnecessarily, standing as far away from him as possible in the tiny room.

Although it was small it was fully equipped and spotless, with a view out into the garden. He wondered if she'd come if he invited her to dinner. He would enjoy cooking for her here.

'Is that your house?' he asked, looking across the gardens.

She nodded. 'Yes. Laura and I have this end.'

He looked at the windows and wondered which room was hers. Would he see her light from here? Or maybe her shadow on the curtains?

He stifled a groan and dragged his eyes away from the window before she could smell a rat.

'What's upstairs?' he asked her, which was nearly as bad.

'Two bedrooms. You can see the sea from the main bedroom,' she told him, and led the way, keeping out of reach. Through a gap in the houses he could see the grey swell of the North Sea, the gulls wheeling low over the surface, the thin winter sun gleaming on their wings.

'It's gorgeous. I love the sea.'

'It's only a glimpse.'

'Even so.' He turned towards her, and she backed away, heading for the door. He stopped her with a hand.

'Jo?'

'Come and see the other bedroom and the bath-room—'

'Jo, come here.'

She stayed where she was, and he dropped his hand. 'Jo, it's OK. I'm not going to jump on you.'

She regarded him warily. 'Last night,' she began, and fizzled out.

'Last night we were intoxicated by the wine and the sea and the night air. Jo, you're safe. Trust me, please. We need to talk about this.'

'About what?' she asked guardedly.

'This—whatever it is—between us. I don't know what it is, or where it came from, but I know you feel it too.' He sat on the edge of the bed and patted the mattress beside him. 'Sit down. Talk to me.'

She sat, but she hardly relaxed. Still, he supposed it was a start.

He sighed inwardly. 'I've got a suggestion. We're both free, there's no reason why we shouldn't get to know each other—'

'We work together—'

'That's how most couples meet. As I was saying, there's no reason why we shouldn't get to know each other—go out together, spend some time together, just see where this thing leads us.'

Jo met his eyes, and there was clear determination in the hazel depths. 'I'm not going to have an affair with you, Ed. I have to live in this town, and bring up my daughter. I have a reputation to preserve—'

'And I don't? Anyway, I'm not suggesting we should make love in broad daylight in the middle of the beach!'

A smile tugged at her mouth, and he almost sighed with relief. Thank God! He'd thought for a moment she'd lost her sense of humour.

'So what are you suggesting? A few drinks, a meal, and then after a decent interval bring me back here and seduce me? My daughter's bedroom overlooks this house.'

'We could always make love in the dark,' he said rashly, but she caught the twinkle in his eye and smiled.

'Ed, I'm serious, I'm not looking for a relationship. I like you, and, yes, I find you attractive, but I've been on my own for years. I'd find any presentable man attractive.'

'Would you?'

'Yes.'

'So attractive that you'd kiss him in the moonlight until your legs turned to jelly and your brain turned to mush?'

'Don't be silly.' She looked down at her hands. Her fingers were twisted together, knotted up. She unravelled them. 'Ed, it won't work.'

'Give it a try—please? I like you, Jo. I'm wary, too. You aren't the only one who's ever been hurt, but sometimes we just have to take a risk.' He reached for her hands, covering them with one of his, squeezing the mangled fingers gently. 'Please?'

She looked up again and in her eyes he could see a sort of yearning, as if she longed to take that risk. 'I don't want to be rushed,' she told him, and the tension seeped out of him like air out of a punctured balloon.

'I won't rush you.' He stood and drew her to her feet. 'Thanks.' He bent, unable to stop himself, and brushed her lips with his. Then he let her go, despite the nagging of his instincts that told him to grab her and hang on tight, and she showed him the bathroom and the other bedroom.

He didn't take any of it in. He wasn't interested, not really. It was clean, pretty, functional—that was all he asked. And, as an unexpected bonus, it was near Jo. Very near. So near she could pop in for coffee or a drink, or—

He yanked his mind up short. No. He'd promised to give her time, and if he started thinking like that he wouldn't give her ten minutes.

He followed her out of the little door and back across the gardens. They found Rebecca in the kitchen surrounded by the delicious aroma of fresh coffee.

'Well? What did you think?' she asked, looking from one to the other.

'I think I sold it to him. Excuse me, I just want to see what Laura's up to. She's got homework to do.'

They watched her go, then Rebecca looked at Ed searchingly for a moment, before smiling. 'So, is it any good?'

'Perfect. I love it,' Ed told her. 'I don't know what rent you want, but if it isn't too outrageous I'm sure I can manage—'

'I don't want anything!' Rebecca said, looking appalled. 'It's empty—have it, dear. I'm going to have to chuck you out before Easter, anyway. No. You have it for nothing, please. It will do it good. You can pay the running expenses.'

'Well, of course I will. Are you sure? That seems absurdly generous...'

She tutted and brushed him aside. 'Don't be silly. It'll be nice to think of someone living in it. I don't think being empty does houses any favours at all. No, you enjoy it. There's a phone, but for incoming calls only, I'm afraid. I expect you could get it connected if you wanted.'

'It would be useful. When can I move in?'

'Oh—well, today, I suppose, if you want. I'll sort out the linen—'

'I've got sheets and towels. I'll use my own, then I won't feel so guilty!'

'Idiot,' she said affectionately. 'I've made coffee—can you stay?'

'That would be lovely. Was that your coffee last night?'

She gave a musical little laugh. 'You guessed. Poor Maurice, his coffee's dreadful. By the way, that was a delicious meal you cooked for us. He was very grateful.'

'My pleasure. It was a very pleasant evening, wasn't it?' he added, fishing for her reactions.

They were everything Maurice would have wanted. 'Lovely,' Rebecca replied, and her eyes seemed to lose focus. 'Really lovely. I felt quite spoilt.'

Ed smiled gently. 'It must be hard, being on your own.'

'Oh, but I'm not. I've got Jo and Laura.'

He said nothing, and she gave a rueful smile. 'You're right, of course. It isn't quite the same. I do miss having a man around—a different perspective. I wish...' She trailed off and gave him a searching look.

'You wish?'

'Nothing. Let's go through to the sitting room—Jo'll probably join us in a minute.'

He doubted it, but it didn't matter. There'd be plenty of other opportunities. He stopped the smile before it took over his face...

'Hi. What brings you here?'

Jo shut the car door, schooling her face into impassivity. She wasn't going to smile, just because he was here—well, only a bit. 'Oh, just a meeting. What about you?'

'Casualty—a query fracture.'

'Ah, well, you'll be lucky. The radiographer's here so you can have pictures.'

'So I gather.' Ed fell into step beside her and her traitorous body seemed to come alive at his nearness. 'How long do you expect to be here?' he asked.

'About an hour. Why?'

He shrugged. 'Just wondered what you were doing about lunch.'

She paused at the door and met his eyes, forcing herself to be sensible. 'Nothing. I don't tend to have lunch.'

'You should. It's bad for you not to eat regularly.'

'I eat regularly. I eat breakfast and supper.' She changed the subject. 'How's the cottage?'

'Fine—lovely. I'm really delighted. I like Maurice a great deal, but it's wonderful to have my own space.'

'I suppose you're used to living alone,' she said.

'Are you fishing for information?'

She coloured. She had been, but she didn't like being caught out so blatantly! 'Not really,' she lied. 'Just passing comment.'

He laughed without humour. 'You're right, of course. I have been alone for a long while—about four years?

My partner at the time decided she didn't want to relocate when I did. She opted for her career.'

Hence his remark yesterday about not being the only one who'd been hurt.

'I'm sorry,' she said softly.

He shrugged. 'That's life. Anyway, there hasn't been anyone significant since. How about you? How long have you been alone?'

'Why are we suddenly talking about me?' she asked, feeling as if he'd pulled the rug out from under her. She had no intention of talking about herself!

'Fair's fair. I told you about me.'

'There's nothing to tell. It's just me and Laura.'

His eyes were searching, touched with curiosity and compassion. 'That's sad,' he said after a pause.

'No, it's tidy. I told you I wasn't looking for a relationship, and I wasn't just saying it. I'm not. We're happy, Ed.' She looked at her watch and pushed the door open. 'I must get on, I'm going to be late. I'll see you round.'

Ed watched her go, wondering what was wrong with all the men in Yoxburgh that a beautiful woman like Jo with a warm personality and a lively sense of humour could still be alone after all this time.

He knew she was, of course. Maurice had been more than happy to talk about Rebecca's family, and yesterday Rebecca had been fairly forthcoming while Ed had sat there like a sponge and blotted it all up. There'd been no man in Jo's life, by all accounts, since she was eighteen and pregnant and had been abandoned by her lover.

And now she was thirty.

Had Laura's father hurt her that much?

He felt a boiling rage towards the unknown deserter who had left her so carelessly. Without her parents her life would have been much harder, and Laura's too. And he thought he'd had problems!

He went into the casualty department and found his patient, a young lad with a slightly bent-looking arm. He smiled reassuringly at the woman beside the boy, and dropped to his haunches in front of them.

'Hello, there,' he said, eyeing the distorted limb. 'I'm Dr Latimer. So, what happened to you?'

'I fell off my bike—are you going to take an X-ray?'

'That's right. Mind if I feel it?'

'It hurts,' the boy said warily.

'I'm sure. Can you wiggle your fingers for me?' Ed asked, and watched carefully as the boy moved them very slightly. They were pink, and when he touched them the boy could feel it all right, so he was confident there was no serious disruption to the nerves or blood supply, despite the slightly strange angle.

'I think we'll need a picture of that before we do any more,' he said. He straightened and smiled at the woman again. 'Are you his mother?'

'That's right—Mona Davies. His name's Richard.'

'OK. Right, well, we need to ask the radiographer to take some pictures of Richard. If it's a fairly simple break we can set it here and plaster it, otherwise he'll have to go to the Audley, I'm afraid.'

'Oh, I do hope you can do it. We haven't got a car at the moment and it's such a long way on the bus.'

'I'll do my best. Right, let's get these X-rays.'

He found the nurse, filled in the X-ray request form and went into the office while he waited.

'Anything else for me while I'm here?'

'A child with a bead up her nose. We can't get hold of it, and she can't blow it out.'

'I'll get it out. Got any superglue and a match?'

'Somewhere. Do you want to do it now?'

'Better, in case she sniffs it up and it goes down into her lungs.'

He was taken over to the little girl, who was sitting on her mother's lap, looking sorrowful.

'This is Mrs Barham—and this is Emily,' the nurse said.

'Hello, there, Emily,' Ed said with a smile. She buried her face in her mother's neck and he switched the smile to the mother. 'Hi. I'm Ed Latimer. I gather she's got a bead up her nose.'

'Yes—it's all my fault. I let her play with a broken necklace. I never thought she'd be silly enough to stick it up her nose.'

'Not silly,' the little one mumbled through her mother's jumper.

'Of course not. It was just an accident, wasn't it? Are you going to let me see it?'

The blotchy little face appeared slowly from the hollow of her mother's shoulder. 'It's up there,' she said, shoving her finger up her left nostril.

'Don't push it,' he cautioned, catching her hand. 'Can you turn round so I can see?'

She swivelled, and he took a pen torch from his pocket and shone it up her snub of a nose. 'Oh, yes— it's a pretty pink one. Right, well, I think I can probably get that out without too much difficulty, but you'll have to lie very still for me. Can you do that?'

She nodded solemnly, and he ruffled her hair and stood. 'I'll just get the gear. Can you come into the treatment room?'

He laid her down, made her promise not to move and put a drop of superglue on the end of a matchstick. Very carefully, he held the end of the matchstick against the bead until it had stuck, then pulled it carefully out.

'There you go! One bead.'

'Can I have it?' she asked.

'So long as you promise not to stick it back up,' he warned, and he handed her the matchstick and bead. 'Now, young lady, remember, you must never stick anything up your nose.'

'Not even my finger?'

He stifled the smile. 'Not even your finger,' he agreed. 'OK.'

'Thank you, Dr Latimer,' Mrs Barham said with a heartfelt smile. 'I'll go and put the rest of the necklace in the bin.'

'Sounds like a good idea, although I think she might have learned her lesson.'

'I hope so!'

He watched them go, then turned back to the nurse. 'How's the X-ray coming on?'

'It's ready.'

'Right, let's go and have a look and see if it's within my scope.'

It was, just about. Given the distance, the discomfort of joggling on the bus and the likelihood of them not doing it any differently in a bigger hospital, Ed decided to have a go.

'I want to pull it out a little straighter so I'll give you an anaesthetic into your arm to make it numb, and then we'll do it.' He turned to the nurse. 'I'll need a compression bandage and lignocaine to numb the arm,' he told her, and then explained to the boy and his mother what he intended to do.

'I'm going to squeeze all the blood out of your hand and wrist, and put some local anaesthetic into the blood vessels. That numbs the area very successfully, better than any other way. Then I can pull the arm straighter, without hurting you, and put the plaster on.'

'It sounds very complicated,' Mona said cautiously.

'It's not. It's fine, really. It's quite time-consuming, but it works. The good thing is there's no nerve damage and the blood vessels are OK, otherwise he would have to go to the Audley.'

They raised his arm, bandaged the hand from the fingertips down to cut off the circulation, put a strap round his arm to prevent any new blood from coming in, then removed the bandage and injected the local anaesthetic.

'Better?' he asked after a few minutes, and Richard nodded.

'It doesn't hurt now.'

'Good. Right, I just want to see if I can straighten it a little.' Ed took hold of his hand, gripped it and the top of the forearm firmly and eased them apart. There was a crunch, and the bones realigned satisfyingly.

'OK?' he checked, and the boy nodded. He looked a little pale, but he wasn't screaming the place down so the anaesthetic must be working.

The arm seemed quite stable so Ed asked for another X-ray to check the alignment. It was as good as he felt he could get it so he took off the strap, let the circulation back into the arm and, once the hand had recovered, he checked the colour and warmth of the fingers.

'Can you feel anything?'

'Yes—it's odd, but I can still feel things a bit.'

'Just not pain.'

'That's right.'

'Good. OK, we'll plaster it.'

It took another half-hour before Ed was happy with Richard's arm, and then he had visits to do. What a good job he hadn't talked Jo into lunch!

The afternoon passed quickly—too quickly. He was back at the practice for evening surgery, and finally he was able to go home at seven.

He was starving—too hungry to cook—and there was

a chippy down the road. He pulled up outside it, bought good old cod and chips, parked the car by the cottage and walked down to the seafront to eat his meal.

He leaned on the sea wall, looking out over the dark water and listening to the low roar of the surf on the shingle. The wind, always present, tugged his hair, and he turned his face to it and closed his eyes. He loved the smell of the sea—the strange mixture of salt and tar and seaweed on the high-water mark.

The food was good—hot and freshly cooked and delicious. He wondered what his patients would think if they could see him eating something so high in fat, but he didn't care. He was hungry, it filled the hole and the fish was highly nutritious.

He screwed up the paper, scrubbing his hands on it, and turned his back to the sea wall. Jo's house was in front of him and slightly to the left, and as he looked he saw a light come on upstairs.

Her room? She'd said Laura's room looked out over the back. Did Jo have a sea view? Probably.

He thought of their kiss, and ached. Was she thinking of him?

A car swept onto the drive of her house, and he recognised it as the evil machine that had nearly given him heart failure. Unable to stay away, he strolled over and stood on the other side of the garden wall, waiting for her to get out.

She smiled and slammed the door. 'Hi. What are you doing?'

'Just finished supper,' he said, holding up the paper so she could see it in the streetlight. 'How about you? Have you eaten?'

'Yes—I've just come back from a visit.'

He leaned on the wall and met her eyes in the strange yellow light. 'Fancy a coffee?'

'Is your coffee as good as your cooking?'

'Better,' he promised.

A smile brushed her lips. 'OK. I'll just tell Mum. Go and put it on. I'll come via the garden.'

He went back and ran an eye over the sitting room. There were still a couple of boxes scattered about, but he'd only been there two days—less. He put the kettle on, warmed the cafetière and made the coffee, lit the gas fire and went to the back door, switching on the outside light.

He was impatient. Excitement thrummed in his veins, a curious buzz of anticipation that he couldn't remember having felt in years. He stood at the door, waiting, and then he heard the creak of the gate and his heart jerked against his ribs.

Jo.

Ed was standing in the garden, by the slightly open door, waiting for her. Her footsteps faltered, but she told herself not to be a fool. He might be attractive, he might be a flirt, he might be all sorts of things, but he was also a gentleman.

It was funny how she knew that. Even knowing him as slightly as she did, she knew she could trust him to keep his word.

And he'd promised not to rush her.

She found herself hurrying down the path towards him, and he reached out with his arm and gathered her in against him for a quick hug before pushing the door open and ushering her into the sitting room.

The gas coal fire was lit, flickering a welcome, and the enticing smell of fresh coffee drifted from the kitchen. 'Have a seat,' he said, and went into the kitchen, emerging a moment later with a tray.

'Smells wonderful. I've been so busy today I've hardly had time to turn round.'

He laughed. 'Tell me about it. That fracture took hours—it's a good job we didn't arrange to meet for lunch.'

'There you go, then. I was right.'

'For the wrong reasons,' he pointed out, and handed her a mug of coffee. 'Shortbread?'

'Home-made?'

He chuckled. 'In which spare minute? No, it's not home-made.'

She had a finger of it anyway. It was her Achilles' heel, and she wondered if he'd known that. She decided as she bit into it that she didn't care.

He stretched out in the chair, and she watched him out of the corner of her eye and wondered what it was about him in particular that made her pulse do silly things.

'Tell me about your day,' he said quietly.

'My day? Oh. Busy. Postnatal checks, a meeting, a couple of antenatal checks, booking someone in. The usual.'

'How's Julie Brown?'

'Fine. The baby's growing like a weed.'

Ed grinned lazily. 'Thought he might. He's got a good appetite. Have another bit of shortbread.'

'You're bad for me,' she told him, reaching out to take another finger. He took one too, and she watched his clean, even white teeth bite into it and had to stop the little sound that tried to erupt from her throat.

For heaven's sake, how could eating a piece of short-bread be so erotic?

She kicked off her shoes and curled her feet under her, cradling her mug and staring into the coffee so she wasn't looking at him. Clearly, watching him wasn't going to do her any good at all so she might as well not do it!

Instead she looked around the room—at the music system he'd got set up in the corner, the books on the shelves, the little touches that made it his.

'It seems really homely,' she said in surprise. 'I mean, we try to make it welcoming but without personal touches it's very difficult.'

'It's lovely. I'm thrilled with it. The bed's brilliant as well. It's big enough, and it's firm enough. I hate saggy beds.'

'So do I,' she said, and wondered how they'd got onto the subject of beds.

Ed unwound himself from the chair, went over to the hi-fi and fiddled through a collection of CDs which was threatening to take over, finally selecting one and putting it on.

Soft, romantic music flowed round Jo, and he topped up her coffee and sat down again, watching her over the rim of his mug. 'How's your mother?'

'She's fine.'

'Maurice can't talk about anything else. I think he's suddenly opened his eyes and seen her for the first time.'

'I know. She's the same.'

'How do you feel about it?'

She shrugged and stared into the fire. 'I don't know. It's odd. She's my mother—it seems really strange to see her flirting with him.'

'It must be.'

'I don't mind,' she added hastily. 'Don't think that. I'm glad for her, it's just...'

'Odd.'

'Yes.'

She set down her coffee-mug and wriggled her feet back into her shoes. 'I have to go. Laura won't do her homework unless I nag, and I don't want her getting to bed too late. You won't forget the panto rehearsal tomorrow night, will you?'

'No, I won't forget.'

'You didn't come yesterday.'

'I was moving. I won't miss any more—not unless I'm on call and I have to go.'

'Get the others to change their rotas for the panto week. You can't slide off during a performance.'

'Yes, miss,' he said dutifully, and she laughed and shook her head.

'I'll see you tomorrow. Thanks for the coffee.'

'My pleasure.' He walked her to the door, and she wondered with a tremor of anticipation whether he'd kiss her goodnight.

For a moment she thought he wouldn't, but as they reached the door he drew her into his arms. 'One last thing,' he murmured, and then his lips touched hers and she was lost.

His mouth was gentle, coaxing, and despite her resolve she parted her lips and kissed him back.

He groaned deep in his throat and his arms tightened, easing her closer. She could feel the pounding of his heart against hers and the slight tremor in his limbs. His chest was heaving under her hands, and then he lifted his head, trailing his lips down the curve of her jaw and taking tiny little bites from the tender skin of her throat.

A helpless moan escaped from her lips, and he returned to them, his mouth gentle, sipping, tasting, driving her wild. She leaned into him and his hands came up and steadied her, easing her away.

'You'd better go,' he said gruffly, and she could see the raw need etched on his face.

She nearly didn't leave. She so, so, nearly stayed, but out of the corner of her eye she caught sight of Laura's bedroom window, and remembered all the reasons this was such a bad idea.

Without a word she turned and opened the door and walked away.

She didn't look back until she was safely inside her own house. Then she went into Laura's empty room, turned off the light and crossed to the window.

He was still standing there, looking up at her, and she closed her eyes and pressed her lips together against the little sound of need. She didn't need him. It was only physical. She'd been fooled like that before, and look what had happened.

She turned away from the window and nearly fell over a heap of discarded clothes dropped in the middle of Laura's floor.

No, there were plenty of reminders of what could happen if she let her heart rule her head. She'd better not let it happen again.

CHAPTER FIVE

JO DIDN'T know how she'd feel with Ed after that kiss but, apart from a quick smile and a wave as he dived into his consulting room, she didn't see him the next day until the afternoon antenatal clinic, and then they were working in tandem anyway so she didn't really see him to speak to until afterwards.

He found her in the kitchen, boiling the kettle and rinsing out the mugs.

'Tea?' she offered brightly.

'Please. Anything interesting to report?'

'No, not really. Everybody's chugging along nicely. Actually, that's not quite true. I've got one baby small for dates—I'm sending her for a scan, but her other two were on the small side so I think it's just the way she does it.'

'Maybe she doesn't have very good placentas. Some women just don't.'

'Maybe. We'll see.' She poured the water into the mugs, mashed the teabags and fished them out. 'Here,' she said, sliding the mugs across the worktop. 'Milk's in the fridge behind you.'

He did the honours and put the milk away, then dropped onto a chair and propped his feet on another. 'What time does the rehearsal start?'

'Seven forty-five—always.'

He nodded. 'I've got a full surgery. Apologise to Roz for me if I'm a bit on the drag, would you? I don't even know if I'm going to be able to stay awake that long.'

He closed his eyes, and she couldn't resist the opportunity to study his face.

It fascinated her. His lashes lay like dark crescents against his cheeks, and she could see the shadow of his beard on his jaw. Her palm remembered the rough scrape of stubble, and she had to stop herself reaching out to touch him—to run her hand over that angular jaw, to trail her fingers over the soft fullness of his lips or trace the laughter lines that bracketed his mouth—

His lids flicked open and their eyes met and held.

'I couldn't sleep last night after you left,' he said quietly. 'The house just seemed—very empty.'

'That's silly,' she told him. 'I'd only been there a few minutes.'

'You underestimate the force of your personality. Believe me, I missed you.'

She felt absurdly pleased. 'You're daft,' she said, and, dipping her finger in the tea, doodled on the table top.

'Just very attracted to you and wondering how to deal with it,' he replied, leaning forward and catching her hand, stilling it. 'I kept thinking about that kiss—about the feel of your lips, and the softness of your mouth, and the intoxicating fragrance of your skin.'

Heat suffused her, and with a little sound of protest she pulled her hand away and stood, going to the sink and rinsing her mug. 'Ed, stop it,' she pleaded quietly. 'Don't do this to us. It isn't fair.'

'Why not?' His voice was right behind her, his breath brushing her ear, teasing her skin. 'You're a beautiful woman, Jo. How can it be wrong to tell you that?'

She spun, ready to tell him off for harrassing her, but the look in his eyes was totally sincere and honest, and the protest died on her lips. 'I'm not beautiful,' she said instead, and could have kicked herself for falling for his charm.

He smiled, a knowing, gentle smile. 'We'll have to agree to differ,' he said, and, putting his mug in the sink, he left her alone with what was left of her brain. She washed out his mug, put it on the draining-board and wiped her hands.

Why was she such a sucker for a pretty line? Surely she'd have learned her lesson by now!

'Right, can I have you all here, please? I want to run through the end of the first half, with Belle meeting the Beast for the first time.'

Ed watched Jo playing the innocent virginal Belle, and as the Beast gathered her into his arms and trod on her toes for the third time he found himself growing more and more frustrated.

'Is there a man here who can dance?' Roz called out. 'I just want someone to show Peter how it's supposed to look.'

There were catcalls and jokes and stupid suggestions, but nobody actually got to their feet.

Ed gave a resigned sigh and moved forward. He could dance, but he wasn't sure if he could hold Jo in his arms and whirl her around, without disgracing himself.

'Ah, Ed,' Roz said with relief. 'Are you volunteering?'

'I don't know if I can do it any better, but I'll have a go. My mother insisted I should learn when I was a child, but I think I've forgotten more than I ever knew.'

'I never knew it,' Peter confessed with a chuckle, 'and if I go on like this Belle will be in a plaster cast on the night.'

'Right—over here. You ask her to dance, you have the little bit of repartee, then she says, ''I would be honoured,'' and you take her in your arms and sweep her off around the stage. OK? Can we have the music, please?'

Ed bowed, Jo curtseyed, he held out his arms, she drifted into them, and then, as if they'd done it for years, they circled the stage, perfectly in tune. When they got back to the front and he bowed, a cheer went up and Peter shook his head.

'Don't suppose you'd like my part, would you? I can't sing, I can't dance—the only reason I got it is because I'm the only one who's taller than her.'

'You just want to get out of learning your lines,' someone called, and everyone laughed.

'Don't involve me in this,' Ed said, throwing up his hands. 'Anyway, you're fine. I was watching you. You're holding her in front of you, instead of slightly to the side. If you hold her like this, her feet are around yours and not under them. Try it.'

He did, and it seemed to work a little better. Ed retreated to the back of the hall and watched, then winced as Peter trod on Jo again.

'Sorry, Belle,' he said heavily. 'I just can't seem to get it.'

'Keep trying,' Roz said cheerfully. 'You aren't going to get out of learning the lines, Peter. Right, everyone, let's have the village scene and Belle and the Beast can go off and practise.'

They met again in the teabreak, and Jo took him on one side. 'Thanks for your help,' she said softly. 'He was getting desperate. He really hasn't ever danced. I'm sure he'll be fine now.'

'How about your toes?' Ed asked her with a grin. 'Will they survive?'

'Just be ready with the aspirin,' she said with a laugh, and then went off to practise some more.

He watched her go, wishing he had been able to be

the Beast. There was a huge part of him that wanted to do it because he wanted to be the one to dance with Belle, he wanted to be the one to hold her, and kiss her, and marry her in the finale.

And maybe not just in the finale.

What a sobering thought.

Anyway, he wasn't an option, in any shape or form.

'Ed?'

He looked up and smiled distractedly. 'Hi, Roz.'

'Thanks for your help just now. You really are turning into an asset. Have you done panto before?'

'Yes, loads of times when I was a child. I just hope I can fit it all in. I really do have a lot of commitments and I don't want to let anybody down because I haven't been able to give it the time it needs.'

'You'll be fine. Having done it before helps, of course. You know how to fit in.'

'Yes, you just heckle the producer, isn't that right?'

Roz laughed and disappeared into the throng, and Laura materialised at his side, hitching herself up onto a table. 'I think you should have been the Beast,' she said without preamble.

He looked down at the mini-Jo, and gave a lopsided smile. 'Why's that?'

'You're much better. You look the part. You need to be good-looking when the mask comes off, and Peter's sweet but he's just not—well, he's no prince, is he? Not enough machismo.'

Ed gave a startled laugh. 'Laura, if you keep on like this my head will get so big I wouldn't get in the mask anyway,' he said with a grin. 'Besides, what does a prince look like?'

'I dunno, but in the absence of a real one I guess you'll do,' she said with a cheeky wink and, slipping off the table, she left him.

'What did she want?'

He looked at Jo and chuckled. 'Me to be the Beast. She says Peter doesn't look like a prince when he takes his mask off.'

'And you do?'

He couldn't stop the smile. 'So your daughter says. I can take a lot of her flattery.'

'You're so susceptible.'

'No, I just know how to take a compliment,' he said, tongue-in-cheek.

Her mouth twitched. 'You'll get swollen-headed.'

'That's what I told her.'

'I'll have to have a word.'

'Spoilsport,' he said.

He looked down at Jo and wondered how in such a short time she could have come to dominate his life to such an extent. Two weeks ago he hadn't even met her, and now for two pins he'd take on a major part in the pantomime just to stop her toes getting crushed!

Jo had a phone call at lunchtime, summoning her to the house of Liz Bateman, the woman whose baby was small for dates. She arrived at two, and the woman opened the door to her in tears.

'It hasn't moved since last night,' she told Jo, and scrubbed at the tears on her cheeks. 'I keep telling myself it's nothing, that I'm just imagining it, but...it seemed to move quite violently for a while, and since then there's been nothing.'

'Oh, dear,' Jo said gently. 'Well, let's not get ahead of ourselves. It might have just worn itself out yesterday and be having a rest. Did you have your scan this morning?'

She shook her head. 'No. Roger wasn't here to drive me, and I was too upset to drive myself.'

'OK.' She looked around the living room, and moved a couple of toys off the settee. 'Just lie here and I'll have a listen.'

She lifted Liz's jumper up and pulled down the front of her trousers to expose the firm curve of her pregnancy. She felt gently for the lie of the baby, and it was quite normal—head down and with the baby's spine pressed against the right side of Liz's abdomen. 'How many weeks are you? Thirty-four?'

'Yes.'

She wasn't big enough, Jo thought again, rummaging for the equipment. 'OK.' Kneeling beside the settee, she spread a little gel on the skin above the baby's back. She turned on her Sonicaid, and ran it over the skin slowly, searching for the heartbeat. After what seemed like an age, she sank back onto her heels and turned it off.

'Liz, I'm sorry, I can't find anything. The battery might be flat. Let me try with the old-fashioned trumpet.'

She took out her wooden Pinard stethoscope, wiped Liz's abdomen dry and pressed one end of the trumpet to where she thought the baby was, putting her ear to the other end.

Nothing. She tried again, felt the lie of the baby once more and made a further attempt, but it was no use.

'It's dead, isn't it?' Liz said quietly.

'I don't know. I can't tell you without a scan, but I am concerned. I think we ought to go in, don't you?'

'But I can't get there.'

'I'll take you. I'll just ring the hospital, if I may?'

'Sure. The phone's in the kitchen. Help yourself.'

Jo stood and went into the kitchen at the back, closing the door behind her before dialling the antenatal unit. 'Hi, it's Jo Halliday here. I've got a query intra-uterine death for scan—I want to bring her in now. Elizabeth Bateman.'

'OK. About half an hour?'

'Something like that. Thirty-four weeks' duration, third baby, first two normal but a bit small. It's small for dates—she was booked for a scan this morning anyway but her husband couldn't bring her.'

'Fine. We'll see you in a bit.'

She hung up the phone and went back into the room. Liz was lying there still, tears coursing down her cheeks.

'I know it's dead,' she said softly.

'You can't be sure. Come on, let's go and have the scan, and we can talk about it when we've got the result.'

Liz nodded and stood, rearranging her clothes absently. 'What about the others? I'd better ring my friend and ask her if she can hang on, and I probably ought to ring Roger.'

'I'll pack up and wait in the car. I've got a couple of phone calls to make anyway. Bring your notes.'

Jo put her things away, went back to the car and rang the surgery. 'I'm taking Mrs Bateman to the Audley for a scan—any calls for me?'

'No. You're the only one, though—the place has gone mad.'

'OK. I'll take the mobile, but if you can get someone else to cover if possible it would be good. I don't want to have to leave her.'

Liz came out at that moment and got into the car, giving Jo a wan smile. 'Come on, then, let's go and get this over with.'

She was silent all the way there, although Jo could practically feel the thoughts coming off her in waves, and when they arrived they were seen almost immediately.

The person who did the scan was very good, patient

and careful to explain what they all already knew in their hearts.

Liz's baby had died because the placenta had failed. 'See, it's quite small. The placenta usually covers a larger area than that, and the baby is very small for its age.'

'I knew it was dead,' Liz said heavily. 'I knew last night. You knew, too, didn't you?' she said to Jo.

'I was fairly sure. It's unusual not to find a heartbeat at this stage. Earlier, maybe, but by now the baby's heartbeat is quite strong and unmistakable. I would have been able to detect it if it was there—and I heard it yesterday.'

'So what happens now?' Liz asked after a pause.

'Now you see the consultant, and he'll arrange for you to come in and have the baby here.'

'Can't I have it at home?'

'We'll talk to him.'

They did, and he explained that it was unlikely that she'd go into labour spontaneously and would probably need to be induced.

'If you do go into labour, I'd still recommend that you come in because obviously it will be quite sad and you'll need a lot of support. Sometimes mothers need quite a lot of pain relief because it can be a fairly negative experience, and we don't want it to be any worse for you that it has to be.'

Liz nodded. 'OK,' she said.

And that was that. She didn't say another word until they were back at her house, and then she turned into Jo's arms and sobbed her heart out. 'Oh, Liz, I'm sorry,' Jo murmured, and rocked her gently until she stopped crying. Then she led her into the kitchen and made them a cup of tea.

'I don't want to go to hospital,' Liz said tearfully over

her tea. 'I want to have it here. It just feels wrong to change everything just because the baby's dead.'

'I can't induce you here, though,' Jo explained.

'Can I wait till Friday? Maybe by then I will have gone into labour.'

It was Wednesday. 'Sure,' Jo said gently. 'It will give you time to get used to the idea, but I'm not sure that you'll start without help so do be prepared for that.'

'But if I did—would you let me have it here?'

Jo nodded slowly. 'If it's what you really want, yes, of course, I'll be with you. Talk to your husband, see what he feels.'

She nodded. 'Will I be able to see it and hold it?'

'Of course—either here or in the hospital. You can spend as long as you want with it.'

'Will it look—funny?'

'Probably not. I expect it will be quite thin, but otherwise it will look quite normal, I would imagine.'

She nodded. 'I think I'll lie down for a while. Thanks for taking me.'

Jo hugged her. 'You're welcome. Will you be all right alone? Can I call Roger for you?'

Liz shook her head. 'I'll ring him—he'll be home soon anyway, I expect. I'll be fine. I'm not going to do anything stupid. I've got two lovely children and a husband who adores me. I'm very lucky. I'm just sad. I'll be all right.'

'OK.' Jo left her sitting in the kitchen with a second cup of tea, and drove slowly back to the surgery. Liz needed time to come to terms with the situation, and Jo was pretty sure she'd be sensible.

'Any messages?' she asked the receptionist.

'No. You've got away with it. How was the mum?'

'Not good,' Jo told her. She didn't want to talk about

it any more. No, that wasn't true—she did, but only to Ed. 'Is Dr Latimer about?'

'You've just missed him—he's gone out on a call. Dr Brady's on call but she was out already and it was urgent so he said he'd cover it. I don't expect him back now until tomorrow.'

'Right.'

Jo went home, ran a bath and sat in it, staring at the wall, until Laura came and banged on the door. 'Grannie says supper's ready and don't forget the panto.'

'I haven't,' she replied, and slid under the water. She wanted to wash away the day, rinse all the sadness off her skin and start again. She needed to talk to Ed. Was he back?

She lifted the corner of the blind and looked out over the garden, but there were no lights on in his cottage. He must still be out on the call.

Oh, well. She'd see him later. She'd just have to hang on…

There was something wrong with Jo. Ed watched her over the script as he tried to learn his lines, and when she looked across and caught his eye he could almost feel her pain.

What on earth had happened? He hadn't been back to the surgery. He'd been involved with a car accident and he'd stayed with the trapped victims until they'd been able to free them, acting as back-up for the paramedics. It had been pretty hectic, not entirely successful and, in the manner of these things, time-consuming.

He'd dived home for a quick shower and he'd only just got to the rehearsal on time. He still hadn't eaten. He'd found a pile of biscuits in the hall kitchen and was munching through them steadily while he watched Jo and stared at his script.

Laura came and found him. 'Hi,' she said with a grin. 'How's it going?'

'Slowly. Is your mum all right?'

Laura looked up at the stage and shrugged. 'Dunno. She's been very quiet since she got in from work. I expect something happened—sometimes it does and then she goes funny for a bit.'

He nodded. 'I wondered. I'll talk to her later.'

'Thanks. I don't suppose you want to test me on my words? I still don't know the songs.'

'Nor do I. I was trying to learn mine.'

'That's easy. Nobody interrupts you. Barry's got the worst part—or the Ugly Sisters. That's difficult.'

'They're funny—they do it very well, don't they?'

'Brilliant. They ad-lib the whole time and put everybody off, but they're fantastic. I love them. You've only got a boring part, really.'

'Hmm. Let's just hope I don't make a complete ass of myself.'

'Oh, go on! It would make it really funny!'

'Thanks.' He swatted Laura round the head with the script, and she laughed and ran off with some of his biscuits.

Then Roz was waving and calling him, and he had to go and put his money where his mouth was and start acting. He felt silly at first, but everyone was so good-natured about it that he soon relaxed into the part.

It was hardly unfamiliar after all his experience in the village panto as a child and, as he got into it, it all came flooding back. If it hadn't been for Jo, he would have enjoyed it.

'That was marvellous!' Roz said to him as he left the stage for their break.

He smiled distractedly and thanked her, then followed Jo out into the entrance.

'Are you OK?'

She looked at him, her arms hugging her waist, and shook her head. 'Not really. Can I talk to you later?'

'Sure. Your place or mine?'

'Yours. It's a patient—I don't want to talk about it with Laura around.'

'OK. I'll go back and put the kettle on. You take Laura home and then join me when you're ready.'

She nodded, but she looked on the verge of tears so he took her back inside, gave her a cup of tea and jollied and joked and talked about the pantomimes he'd done as a child to distract her.

Finally it was over, and he went back and waited for her.

She wasn't long. She walked through the door into his outstretched arms and howled her eyes out. Then she hiccuped to a halt, scrubbed her cheeks on her sleeve and sniffed. 'Got a tissue?'

'Kitchen roll?'

She sniffed again, and he followed her into the kitchen and opened a bottle of wine. 'Here,' he said, and handed her a glass. 'Now, come and sit down and tell Uncle Ed all about it.'

She trailed after him, sat beside him on the settee and told him the sorry tale of Liz Bateman's baby.

'She wants to have it at home. I really want to let her, but only if you'll support it and be there too, and she does know the chances are she won't be able to.'

He pursed his lips and stared at the fire. 'Is it wise? They can often give up pushing, get disheartened. What were her other deliveries like?'

'First was normal, in the Audley, the second she had here in the GP unit. This one was planned for home.'

He shrugged. 'I'll be guided by you. As you say, it

may not happen. Now, drink up. You need another glass of that.'

She shook her head. 'No, I'm only having one. I've told her to call me at any time if she wants to, and I don't want to let her down.'

She put the glass down and looked at him. 'Ed?'

'What is it?'

'Will you hold me?'

He let his breath out on a sigh and reached for her, drawing her into his arms. 'Poor baby. Have you had an awful day?'

'Not as bad as Liz Bateman.'

'No. Oh, well, at least you were there for her.'

'I keep wondering if I'd picked it up earlier, if the baby would have been all right...'

He hugged her shaking shoulders and wished there was something he could do to take away the pain. 'How could you have picked it up earlier? These things are often quite sudden—the placenta just packs up and that's that. You can only pick it up when the baby fails to grow enough, and it takes time to see that. You can't scan everyone all the time—it just isn't practical.'

'I know that,' she sniffed, and scrubbed her nose again. 'Oh, I'm being silly. It was just a horrible day.'

'They happen. Mine wasn't brilliant. I sat by the side of the road and held someone's hand while he died. Sometimes that's all you can do.' The man's face swam in front of him, and he squeezed his eyes shut.

'I'm sorry,' she said softly. 'I'm going on about my patient and you've had a grim day as well.'

'Still, it isn't all bad. Peter didn't tread on your toes tonight.'

'No.' She gave a half-hearted little laugh. 'No, he didn't, thanks to you. He's very grateful—and so am I!'

'Good. At least someone's happy.'

He hugged her closer, snuggling down into the corner and pulling her over so she sprawled against his side. 'I ought to go home,' she mumbled sleepily.

'Stay for a while. We both need a hug.'

'Mmm.' She cuddled against him, her head on his chest, and within moments she was asleep. He left her there and sat, sifting her hair through his fingers and remembering the details of his day, until in the end he drifted off as well.

They were woken by the sound of her mobile phone. Jo struggled to her feet, grabbed it from her bag and answered it.

'Right. OK. I'll come now. That's OK.'

She switched it off and looked at him. 'Liz Bateman's in labour. I'd better go and tell Mum.'

'I'll come with you,' Ed said, and, pulling on his coat, he flicked off the lights, locked the door behind them and followed her down the path.

It was a solemn but beautiful birth. The baby was a girl, very small, very thin, but quite perfect, and Liz held her and cried. Jo finished the delivery and shook her head over the size of the placenta. One half of it was shrivelled and withered, the other half very small to support a growing baby.

The vicar came and baptised the baby and they all cried, even Ed. Jo was glad to see him cry. Nobody she would want to know could have been unmoved by it.

She drew him aside and left the couple with their baby and the vicar.

'I need a cup of tea,' she told him, taking him downstairs.

'Me, too. Thank God it was an easy labour.'

'I thought it would be. I'm so glad I let her stay.'

'What happens now?'

She shrugged. 'When they're ready the baby and the placenta need to go to the hospital for examination to find out why she died, but it's obvious, really. Then they'll have a funeral, and start all over again, I expect.'

He nodded. 'Yes. Probably. I don't know where women find their strength. She's been marvellous.'

'She's a mother. That's what it means.'

Ed swallowed. 'Yes, I suppose you're right.' He gave her a hug, then patted her shoulder. 'Shall we take the tea up?'

'Good idea. We could be here for hours. Do you want to go?'

He shook his head, to her relief. 'I'll stay with you, if you want me to.'

'Don't you mind?'

'No. No, Jo, I don't mind.'

'Thanks.'

She gave a half-hearted smile, and he reached out for her hand and squeezed it. 'That's what friends are for.'

It was dawn before they went home. They turned into the drive as the sun crawled over the horizon, and by tacit consent they stood on the sea wall and thought about the night. Ed's arm was firm around Jo, and she leaned her head against his shoulder and gazed sightlessly out to sea.

'You OK?' he asked softly.

'I'll live. Thanks for being with me.'

'Any time.'

He turned her into his arms, cupped her face in his hands and placed a feathery kiss on her lips.

'Why don't you go to bed?'

'It's time to get up—I have to get Laura off to school.'

'Do you have a clinic?'

She shook her head. 'Just some baby visits.'

'Try and get your head down—that's an order.'

She dredged up a smile. 'Yes, sir.'

'That's it. Chin up, you're doing a grand job,' he said softly, and, kissing her again, he left her there and walked swiftly down the little alley and round the corner out of sight.

A moment later her mother joined her.

'Are you all right?'

She turned to her and smiled tiredly. 'I will be.'

'Kettle's on. Come on,' she said gently. She put her arm round her daughter's shoulders, and led her into the house.

CHAPTER SIX

'Jo? IT's Moira Clarke. I'm sorry to ring you so early but I've been feeling ill all night. Hal's away, and the kids are playing up, and I just can't cope…' She paused, and Jo could hear her fighting tears at the other end.

'Don't worry, Moira, I'm on my way. You just lie down and rest, and I'll be with you.'

She tugged on her clothes, grabbed her mobile phone, changed the battery and ran downstairs. There was no time for a hot drink so she filled a glass from the tap and took a swig, scribbled a note to her mother and Laura and ran out.

Moira lived up the coast a little way, in a house almost on the beach. It was isolated, beautiful and in almost permanent danger of flooding, but the Clarkes loved it. Jo loved it too, but she wouldn't live there, especially not with three boisterous boys and another baby on the way.

Please, God, don't let it be another tragedy, she prayed. The Batemans' baby was still in her thoughts every waking moment, and the prospect of another such disaster filled her with dread.

It also made her drive even faster, but at six o'clock on a Saturday morning that probably didn't matter. There weren't a lot of cars about, but she gave the odd rabbit a fright.

She slithered to a halt in the drive of Driftwood Cottage, grabbed her bag and phone and ran to the door.

It was opened by a six-year-old ragamuffin, with spiky blond hair and gappy teeth and a runny nose. 'Mum's in bed,' he told her, without taking his eyes off the Gameboy in his hand. 'She's been chucking up.'

'Thanks, Oliver.' She ran up, forcing herself to go slowly into the room and be calm. Moira was lying on the bed, her eyes closed, a bowl clutched to her chest.

'You look a bit peaky.'

Her eyes opened and she looked at Jo and groaned. 'I feel dreadful. I can't understand it. I just feel—I don't know, off colour somehow. Oliver, turn that thing off!'

The sound of the Gameboy faded into the distance, and Moira dropped her head back and sighed.

Jo put her bag down and frowned. This wasn't a tragedy—this was, unless she was very much mistaken, a woman in labour! 'Have you had any contractions?' she asked, dropping her coat on the chair and rolling up her sleeves.

'No—well, only the practice ones.'

'I'll just wash my hands—I want to have a look at you. Can you slip your things off?'

She went into the bathroom and washed her hands, found a clean towel in the airing cupboard and dried them, then took another towel back with her. Seconds later she was glad she had because there was a gush of fluid and Moira's waters broke.

Jo smiled in relief and mopped with the towels. 'I thought so. You're in labour, my love.'

'But I can't be! It's not due for two weeks, and Hal's away in Germany!'

'Sorry—I think this baby's coming now. And I'll tell you something else—I don't think I've got time to get my box out of the car. Let's have a look.'

She pulled some gloves on with a snap, felt Moira's cervix and rolled her eyes.

'Do you know why you're feeling so horrible? You're in transition. Any moment now you'll be throwing a paddy and then we'll be in business. Mind if I use your phone?'

'Go ahead,' Moira said, sounding and looking shocked. 'It's not due yet! I can't be in labour!'

'Ed?'

'Jo? What is it?' he mumbled, fighting sleep. She had a pang of guilt about waking him when he wasn't on call, but he wanted experience.

'Can you come? I've got a home delivery for you— head north out of town on the coast road, and after about two miles there's a white cottage nearly on the beach— Driftwood Cottage. That's it. Can you come quickly? This one's in a hurry.'

'Aren't they all? Hasn't anyone in Suffolk heard of a nice, steady labour?' he grumbled gently.

'Thanks.'

She cradled the phone, a silly smile on her lips, and turned back to Moira. 'Dr Latimer's coming, too. Have you met him?'

'I've got an appointment with him for Tuesday.'

'Well, you won't need it. Right, let's get the bed stripped. Have you got a sheet of plastic?'

'It's on the bed, under a layer of towels. My labours always start with my waters so I've learned my lesson!'

'In which case, let's just leave you there and put some pads under you to make it more comfy for now. Do you want to walk round?'

'The only thing I really want is a drink, I'm so thirsty— Oh, golly, I can feel a contraction now. Jo, do you think I ought to go to hospital? Perhaps I'd better pack—can you give me a hand?'

Moira flailed her arms, trying to get to her feet, and Jo smiled to herself and helped her up. 'Just walk round for a moment to let it ease. That's it, lean on me—lovely, well done.'

'Jo, I want to go to hospital,' she said, sounding fretful. 'Please, call an ambulance. I need to go. I can't do this here without Hal.'

'Sorry, my love, you've got no choice. Come on, keep going, you'll be fine.'

'Dammit, listen to me! I'm not staying here!' she shouted, and burst into tears. The next moment she was reaching for the sick bowl, and Jo held her and walked her round and soothed her.

Then she handed back the bowl to Jo, smiled weakly and apologised.

'Sorry—transition,' she said. 'I'll be good now.'

Jo laughed. 'I thought you were going to walk to the hospital,' she said.

'So did I. Oh, here we go...Oh, Jo, I want to push.'

'OK. Let me check your cervix is fully dilated—'

'No. I have to push, I *have* to...'

She knelt and leaned over the bed, then with a groan she pushed down and Jo saw the baby's head crowning.

'We're there, Moira. Just pant—that's a good girl. Lovely. Nice and steady... Oh, yes, little one, hello. Welcome to the world.'

Moira turned and sank to the floor, and Jo whisked a towel under her, laid the squalling baby over her leg and glanced up.

'Oh, look, it's the cavalry,' she said, and smiled at Ed.

'Thanks for coming.'

He leant on his car door. 'My pleasure. Sorry I was too late to help. Lovely baby.'

'And a girl, to boot. They will be pleased. They've got three boys, and they're monsters.'

'Little boys always are—and little girls get worse as they get older.'

She chuckled. 'Sounds about right. Oh, it's the most gorgeous day.' She looked around at the sea and the sky and the heathland behind, and wondered what she had done to deserve it all. 'I love it here.'

'It is beautiful, isn't it? We ought to go for a walk—take advantage of it. It'll probably snow next week.'

'Good idea. I tell you what, I have an antenatal check to do on someone in the forest—do you want to come? They're travellers, and I want to try and talk sense into her because she wants a home delivery and they've got no power, no water, no nothing.'

'Brilliant. Sounds like the perfect scenario,' he said drily. 'I suppose you want me to come in and play the heavy uncle?'

She chuckled. 'Sort of. Perhaps a word in her ear? It's a lovely spot,' she added. 'We could go for that walk.'

'Mmm,' he said, but he didn't sound convinced.

Jo had a pang of conscience about hijacking his Saturday morning off, and said so.

Ed gave a wry grin. 'I wasn't doing anything—well, I was asleep when you phoned, but let's just say I had no plans to do anything. I could do with breakfast, though, before we go out. How about coming round for coffee and croissants? The bakery should be open.'

'Good idea, but why don't you come to me? I ought to see Laura and Mum before I go off out for the day—perhaps Laura could come for the walk too?' she suggested, and then wondered if that would put him off. Apparently not. He nodded his agreement without hesitation.

'Sure. Will she be happy to hang around while we talk to your traveller?'

'I don't know. We'll ask her. I'll see you at home.'

'I'll get the croissants.'

She smiled. 'I'll make the coffee.'

They set off down the coast road at a much more reasonable speed, and Jo found herself singing.

She was happy. Moira's baby was fine, her sister was with her now and would stay until Hal got back from Germany, the sun was shining, Ed was coming round for breakfast—the world was looking brighter than it had for ages.

And Ed was going with her to talk sense into Mel.

What more could she want?

'There it is, up ahead there by the edge of the trees, I think,' Jo said. 'We could park here and walk.'

Ed pulled off onto the side of the road, cut the engine and looked at Jo. 'Tell me what you know about her.'

'She's twenty-eight, lives on income support with her partner, no fixed abode unless you count this—and seems quite contented.'

'Health?'

Jo shrugged. 'She seems very well. She's a vegetarian, but I think she eats sensibly. She certainly looks in good condition—hair, skin, that sort of thing.'

'It must be all the fresh air,' Ed said drily. 'OK. Let's go and meet Mel and her other half and find out what's in store for us.'

They left the car and strolled along the sandy track through the heather. It was a lovely morning for a walk, but Laura had declined to come. She had a better offer from Cara, and they'd gone off on the bus to the cinema. How she could shut herself up on such a lovely day Jo didn't know, but kids would be kids.

'This lot look a bit unfriendly,' Ed murmured, drawing her attention to the encampment up ahead. A group of four coaches, lorries and old caravans were clustered together around a central area. A fire smouldered in the middle, an old mattress hanging half out of it, charred and blackened, and a few mangy dogs detached themselves from the shelter of the vehicles and ran towards them.

Moments later they were surrounded by the barking dogs, their fangs bared, their welcome none too friendly. Grubby curtains twitched, and Jo felt the hair rise on the back of her neck.

A man appeared in the doorway of one of the battered old coaches, dressed in combat trousers, boots and a tattered sweater. He swore at the dogs and they subsided, growling instead from a distance.

'Hello,' Jo called, dredging up a smile. 'I'm looking for Mel Jenkins. Is she here?'

'Who wants her?'

'I'm the midwife.'

The man looked searchingly at her, then stepped down from the coach and stood, facing them, his arms folded and his legs slightly apart. It was meant to be intimidating, and it worked.

He jerked his head at Ed. 'Who's he?'

'Dr Latimer—my colleague.'

His eyes flicked over Ed and came back to rest on Jo. They were the coldest, hardest eyes she'd ever seen, and she instinctively moved closer to Ed.

'They don't live here,' the man said.

A woman pushed past him and came out, a baby dangling on her hip. She had a black eye and a yellow bruise on her lip. 'She's up the track about half a mile. They've got an old caravan parked at the edge of the trees. She's all right, isn't she?'

'As far as I know,' Jo confirmed. 'I was just coming to do a routine home visit—I always do when I get a new patient.'

The woman nodded. 'Just go up here and fork left at the pit. You can't miss them.'

'Thanks.'

She disappeared back inside, but the man stayed, watching them with those cold, hard eyes as they walked away.

'Nice man,' Ed said softly. 'I wouldn't want to meet him on a dark night.'

'No. Let's hope we can talk sense into Mel so we don't have to! Did you see her bruises?'

'Yes—and the baby's. I think we ought to report them.'

'I'll contact the liaison officer—I know him,' Jo said. 'He'll keep an eye out.'

They followed the track, and suddenly came to a little clearing. An old caravan with questionable suspension stood at the back of the clearing, and there was a lean-to built at one end of it. A battered pick-up was parked beside it, with a dog in the back. It jumped down and barked but, unlike the others, it wagged its tail and seemed friendly.

Ed bent and held out his hand, and the dog ran up, wiggling its rear end and sniffing him.

'Mel?' Jo called. 'Mel, are you here?'

The door of the caravan opened and a man appeared. Here we go again, Jo, thought, but he stepped down and came over to them with a smile.

'Gizmo, come here,' he said, and the dog ran to his side, tongue lolling. 'Can I help you?' the man asked, and Jo was surprised at how well spoken he was.

'I'm looking for Mel. I'm the midwife—Jo Halliday. I just wanted to come and say hi and find out where she is, in case she needs me urgently, so I can find her in a hurry.'

He smiled and held out his hand. 'I'm Andy Roarke— her partner.' Jo shook his hand, and his grip was firm and straightforward. She felt happier—marginally.

'This is my colleague, Ed Latimer. He's the GP in charge of obstetrics in our practice.'

Andy Roarke shook his hand, too. 'Hi, Ed. She's inside. Come on in.' He opened the door and led them in, and Jo was surprised to find it clean and tidy and organised.

'Visitors, Mel,' Andy said. 'The midwife and the doctor.'

'Oh, hi, Jo. Come in. There's tea in the pot—Andy, could you?'

Mel was sitting with her feet up on a caravan-type bench seat, a steaming cup of tea on the table beside her, and she tried to struggle up.

'Stay there,' Jo told her. 'We're fine.'

She subsided again, and Andy cleared some papers off the other end of the bench so they could sit down. 'Have a pew. How do you take your tea? Milk and sugar?'

Jo could see Ed eyeing the sink and weighing up the possibility of catching something, but she was used to far worse than this. 'Just white, both of us, thanks. I hope you don't mind us popping in—it's just a routine visit so we know where you are in case you have a problem in the middle of the night.'

Mel's face lost some of its tension. 'I wondered,' she confessed. 'I thought maybe you'd come because the social services liaison officer had been on to you—they keep telling me I ought to go into a council flat or something. They just don't seem to be able to accept that we've chosen this lifestyle quite deliberately, and our baby's going to be safe.'

Andy sat beside her, sliding the mugs of tea across the table. 'We used to live in London,' he told them. 'I was an interior designer, Mel had a soft-furnishing business—that was how we met. Things just got too tight, and we were chasing smaller and smaller margins, and then one day we sat back and said, ''What the hell are we doing this for?'' We were miserable.'

'So we stopped, sold everything we had and bought the van and the pick-up, and here we are,' Mel said, smiling affectionately at him. 'Andy does odd jobs and a bit of drawing for a local firm just to keep us ticking over, and I make tie-dye cushions and shawls and things for a craft market, and we get by. I know it's a cop-out, but we're happy.'

Jo laughed softly. 'I can see the pull. Sometimes things just get on top of you, don't they? Most people don't have the guts to get out.'

'We had to. We were talking about a suicide pact—only jokingly, but it brought it home to us.'

Jo nodded. 'So, what are your plans for the baby?'

They looked at each other, then back to Jo. Mel's eyes seemed a little shifty suddenly. 'Well, I have to go to hospital, don't I?'

'No. Not necessarily.'

Her eyes lit up. 'I don't?'

Jo shook her head. 'No. I'd like you to because out here you've got no electricity, no running water, no proper heating—it must get damp with the gas heaters. I can remember caravanning with my parents as a child, and the windows used to stream when we cooked. Your baby's due—when? March?'

'Yes. It'll be warmer then, and we can have the windows open.' She looked down at her hands. 'Jo, I really want to have it here. It's so beautiful in the forest—if the weather's nice I'd like to have it outside, just surrounded by nature. I think that would be so beautiful, don't you?'

Jo sighed inwardly. 'Yes, I do—in theory. But what if it's raining? What if it's cold? What if it's night-time?'

'Lots of babies are born by candlelight. I'd hate harsh electric lights and my feet up in stirrups and men poking me around—'

'Hey, hey, hang on!' Jo said with a laugh. 'It's not like that! My deliveries are all very calm and low-key and beautiful. There's no harsh light or stirrups or anything awful.'

Mel's eyes flicked to Ed, who had remained silent, and he smiled ruefully. 'I'm just there for insurance. She's the midwife, she does the delivery. I have yet to attend a labour where there was time for me to do more than take my coat off before it was all over! I just get handed the baby and told to hold it.'

'What a shame,' Jo teased. 'You see, we really don't aim for high-tech labour. Women were designed to give birth. I'm here just to make sure it's as safe as possible for them to do it.'

'Look, I've been reading about it,' Mel said. 'I'm young, it's my first pregnancy, I haven't had any problems, my mother didn't have any problems—there shouldn't be any reason why I can't give birth at home.'

Jo nodded. 'I agree. I have reservations, though, about you giving birth here. The lack of running water, particularly, worries me. How do you get water?'

'There's a standpipe down at the other settlement,' Andy told them. 'I carry it. African women have done it for centuries, I'm sure I can manage with the help of the pick-up.'

'And electricity?'

'We've got a light that runs off a battery. It's not brilliant, but it works. We use it for emergencies—it's a car inspection lamp.'

'I know the sort of thing,' Ed said. 'I've got one. They're quite effective, but not ideal.'

Mel twisted her fingers, then looked up at Jo challengingly. 'If we can't agree, and I go into labour and won't go to hospital, does that mean you won't come and help me?'

Jo shook her head slowly. 'No, of course not. You're still my patient. Of course I'll come and help—but you have to understand that if, when I get here, I think there's the slightest danger that things are going wrong, I'll want to transfer you to the consultant unit immediately. You've got to agree to that.'

'Just because we're out here?'

'No. It's the same for any home birth. If it starts to go pear-shaped, we give up. I won't let you compromise your baby's life, and I'm sure you wouldn't want me to. I want things to go well for you, and I don't want to interfere unnecessarily, but you've got to trust my judgement.'

Mel nodded. 'So you'll let me try?'

'I want to know the moment you're in labour. I want to check you, check the baby, see if I feel I can work with you under these conditions—there's always the option of the GP unit.'

'But that hasn't got any special facilities, has it?'

'No—just light and heat and running water.'

Mel smiled. 'We can make it warm and light, and Andy can run with the water!'

Ed chuckled, then his face sobered. 'You're really determined, aren't you?'

'It's what we want,' Andy said. 'It's the way we want our baby to start its life. Everybody thinks we're crazy, but it's our life and this is how we want to lead it.'

Ed nodded slowly. 'I don't think you're crazy,' he said. 'I think you're doing what's right for you, but I have to endorse what Jo's saying. If at any time either of us feel that things are getting out of hand, you must agree to be guided by us.'

'And if we don't?'

'Then there's a good chance your baby will suffer,' Jo said calmly. 'I don't panic. If I can deal with a problem, I will. I just know when things aren't right and I need more help. If you choose to ignore that, you'll have to choose to accept the consequences.'

Andy nodded. 'OK. Thanks.'

Jo and Ed stood. 'Just one last thing,' Jo said with a smile. 'If you've got to have it here, can you try and have it in daylight, please?'

Mel chuckled. 'I'll do my best. Thanks, Jo.'

Andy saw them out, and paused at the foot of the steps. 'Mind that lot down there. There's a strange bloke—hard-looking. He's not very friendly.'

'We've met,' Jo said drily, remembering the man with a shiver.

'Ah. Well, steer clear of him. He's a bit dangerous. We're going to move on once the baby's born—get away from him. He makes Mel nervous.'

'I can understand that,' Jo agreed. 'He's got odd eyes.'

'Dead eyes. He gives me the creeps, but he hasn't done anything to us, and so long as he's left alone he's OK, they say.' He lifted his hand. 'Cheers, now. Thanks for coming by. We'll keep in touch.'

They walked back down the track, steering well clear of the other group of travellers.

'Well?' Ed said as they got back to the car.

Jo sighed, rehashing the conversation in her mind. 'I think there's no point in trying to persuade them. They're clearly highly intelligent, educated people. They're just a bit off the wall. If it's what they want, we can't do anything about it. We can hardly section them under the Mental Health Act and lock them up till it's over, can we?'

Ed laughed. 'Probably not. She looks well, though, as

you say. I don't anticipate problems. Have you done a pelvic assessment?'

'Not yet. I think it'll be fine, though. I'll do it when she's nearer. There's no point yet—the baby's still going to grow.'

Ed started the car, and Jo dropped her head back against the headrest and sighed.

'Tired?'

'A bit. I'm glad Laura wasn't here in the end. It made it easier to talk to them.'

'Not that it did a lot of good.'

'Oh, I don't know.' She rolled her head towards him and smiled. 'Thanks for coming with me.'

'My pleasure. As you said, it's a good idea to know where they are in case of problems. I don't like the look of their neighbours.'

'No. I'll talk to the liaison guy.'

'Right, where are we going for this walk?'

'Walk?' Jo said, surprised.

'Yes, walk. You don't call that feeble little stroll a walk, do you?'

Jo groaned and wondered why she'd suggested it. He was obviously a fitness fanatic.

'Seascape or landscape?'

'Can we have both?'

She nodded. 'We'll go up the coast to Dunwich. It'll be windy,' she warned him.

'I can cope. And you'll be all right—you'll just walk in front of me!'

She felt the grin, but couldn't stop it.

'Which way?'

'Left.'

They left the car in a car park, and walked along the top of the shingle bank for miles. There was hardly a soul about, and the wind tugged their hair and froze their ears and cheeks. She found Ed's arm round her shoulder, her hip against his, and his head bent close to hers.

They strolled along in silence for a while, enjoying the sun and the wind and the sea, and then suddenly Ed spoke.

'Tell me about Laura,' he said softly.

She stumbled. 'Laura? What about her?'

'Oh, all sorts of things. How you came to have her, for instance. How you coped alone. Why you're so wary.'

Jo swallowed and caught her lip in her teeth. She hated talking about it, but she supposed he had a right to know if they were getting this close.

'I was seventeen,' she told him. 'I was just about to do my A levels. Richard was twenty-five, mature, witty, rich—at least, he seemed rich to me, compared to the other boys I'd been out with. He smoked French cigarettes, he drank gin and tonic, not beer, he flattered me— told me I was beautiful and that he loved me.'

'And you fell for it.'

'Oh, yes,' she said with a bitter laugh, remembering the impressionable girl she'd been. 'Hook, line and sinker. He told me he was divorced, that his wife hadn't understood him and she'd lied to him. She had two children from another relationship, and she didn't love him any more—you know the sort of thing.'

She could feel Ed stiffening. 'Yes, I know,' he said quietly. 'So what happened?'

'I became pregnant, and I told him. I was sure he'd be delighted because he'd said he'd wished his wife's children had been his own.'

'And they were, of course.'

'Of course. They weren't divorced at all. She lived in London, and was waiting for him to find them a house up here. He went back to her. I never saw him again.'

Ed was silent for a while, just the tension in his arm around her shoulder indicating to her he was angry.

'Bastard,' he said softly, after an age. Then he brought her to a halt, and turned her into his arms. 'I am not married,' he told her very clearly, 'and I never have been. I have no children. I am not a liar.'

She smiled at his vehemence, and reached out to touch his cheek to reassure him. 'No. I know.'

He hugged her gently. 'I'm sorry.'

'I'm not,' she told him honestly. 'I've got Laura and I can't imagine life without her. She is, without exception, the best thing that's ever happened to me, and I can't bring myself to regret her.'

Ed smiled. 'I like her, too. She's got lots of character.'

Jo rolled her eyes. 'Too much. Still, I'd rather have it that way.'

She shivered, and he pulled her back into the shelter of his arm. 'Come on, let's go back,' he said softly, and she felt cherished and cared-for and protected. It was scary how good it felt…

CHAPTER SEVEN

Jo's simple story of her betrayal and abandonment stayed with Ed vividly. He was busy at work, coping with the rash of new cases of flu, going out on visits and driving around hopelessly lost trying to find the patients' houses or dealing with minor casualties at the hospital, and all the time her words rang in his head.

The most significant thing she'd said had been that she wasn't sorry she'd had Laura. To have a child at eighteen must have played havoc with her plans for the future, and yet here she was, twelve years down the line, saying her daughter was the best thing that had ever happened to her.

Ed found that immensely heartwarming, but it didn't really surprise him. He'd seen enough of Jo to know that no baby could be anything but a joy to her, and her obvious grief at the loss of Liz Bateman's baby had been just another part of the woman that she was.

Of course she didn't regret her daughter's birth. How could she? It wasn't in her. No, she would selflessly deny her own wants and needs to give her child the life she felt she should have—it was probably why she was still alone.

That, and a natural wariness about men, which Ed couldn't blame her for. A man like that would put most women off for ever.

It was a crying shame, he thought, watching her at one of the panto rehearsals. She was such a warm and giving person, she'd make a wonderful wife and mother. She was naturally very friendly and open, and she brought a smile to so many faces with her cheerful greet-ings.

She knew everyone, of course, and everyone knew her. It reminded him of the village he'd grown up in, and he felt suddenly homesick for that warmth and wel-come—and for the warmth of Jo's arms.

Then she looked up and caught his eye, and her smile extended to him, drawing him into the group and warm-ing him.

Jo was irresistible.

And Ed was perilously close to falling for her.

A shadow seemed to hover over him. Would she want him? When the chips were down would she still be there, or would she, too, turn away?

'Right, village scene again,' Roz called, 'and can we have a little more enthusiasm, please? We've only got three more rehearsals before the final dress rehearsal, you know!'

He put thoughts of Jo and the future away. There would be time for that later. Just now he had to go back a hundred years or so in time and be jolly.

He gave a quiet snort, shrugged himself away from the wall and joined the others on stage.

Ed seemed preoccupied, Jo thought. He was very busy. Maurice and the others had obviously decided he could cope, and any gentle introduction was now well and truly over. He'd been chucked in at the deep end, and she'd hardly seen him since the day they'd visited Mel and she'd told him about Richard.

That had been three weeks ago, and their duty rotas, Laura's commitments and the rehearsals for the panto seemed to have contrived to keep them apart.

He came up to her at the end of the rehearsal and gave a diffident smile. 'Are you busy now?'

She glanced at her watch. It was ten-thirty already, and they weren't home yet. 'What did you have in mind?'

'Coffee, listening to some music, relaxing.'

She smiled. 'I was going to relax in bed,' she said, and his mouth quirked.

'Sounds good.'

'Alone,' she said repressively, squashing her smile, and he grinned.

'Shame. Can I talk you into being a dirty stop-out for half an hour? I can't remember when we last spent any time alone together. It seems like ages.'

'I know.' She looked round at Laura, who was chatting to friends. As she watched, Laura yawned hugely, and Jo had a pang of conscience. 'I ought to get her home to bed. She's shattered, and I think she's getting a cold.'

'Come round later.'

She nearly said no. She thought of all the good reasons why it was stupid, but then she met his eyes and her resistance disintegrated.

'OK,' she said softly. 'I won't stay long, though.'

'That's all right. I'll light the fire and make the coffee and wait for you.'

'Hi, guys!' Laura ambled up to them, stifling another yawn, and leaned on her mother's shoulder. 'I'm tired,' she said. 'Can we go home?'

'Yes.' Jo didn't mention going round to Ed's. It didn't seem necessary or sensible. She met his eyes over Laura's head and read the promise in them, and wondered if she was totally mad.

Laura went straight to bed and crashed out, but it was still after eleven o'clock before Jo left. She went to tell her mother she was going out, and she eyed her daughter's coat curiously.

'I didn't think you were on call tonight.'

'I'm not. Ed asked me for coffee.'

Her mother's eyes searched her face, and she smiled understandingly. 'OK. I'm off to bed. I'll see you in the morning. Don't be too late.'

Jo thought it was probably already too late, but too late for what? She let herself out, slipping across the gardens and in through Ed's back door. He was there, waiting, with a hug, and she sank into the warmth of his arms with a sigh of relief.

'I've missed you,' he murmured. 'It's been ages since I've held you. I haven't seen you alone for weeks.'

'I know.' She snuggled into his shoulder and sighed again. 'I've missed you, too,' she confessed, letting down her guard a little. His arms tightened, hugging her closer, then he released her and led her over to the settee in front of the fire.

A fresh pot of coffee sat on a tray, with shortbread and cheese and biscuits and other titbits, and she noticed there was soft, romantic music playing in the background.

A scene set for seduction, she asked herself, or just a friend entertaining in a welcoming manner?

Or both? She decided it didn't matter. She was tired, and it was very pleasant, sitting there with Ed. She sipped her coffee and stopped trying to analyse his motives.

'You OK?' he asked softly.

'Mmm. Tired. Don't be surprised if I doze off on you.'

He chuckled. 'Be my guest.'

Ed's fingers trailed over her shoulder, tormenting her with the delicate touch. He was turned half-sideways on the settee, one knee hitched up, his foot tucked under the other thigh. His arms were spread along the side and back, and he looked masculine and a little dangerous. His eyes regarded her steadily.

'I wish we could find more time to be together,' he said in a low voice, his fingers circling slowly. 'Time alone, without the rest of the cast or the other members of the practice or a clinic full of patients.'

'Quality time,' Jo murmured. His touch was like a drug, almost hypnotic in its effect.

'Just quiet time. We're always so busy—there's never time just to sit and be together. No time to talk.'

She turned her head towards him. 'What do you want to talk about?'

A shadow seemed to cross his face. 'Us? There's still so much we don't know about each other.'

It was true. She knew hardly anything about him, but it didn't seem to matter. He'd told her what she needed to know, and the rest was just the icing on the cake. She could do without the icing. Richard had been all icing, and under it the cake had been rotten to the core.

'I know all I need to know about you,' she said softly.

'No, you don't.'

'I do. I know you won't lie to me.'

His fingers drifted up the side of her neck to her jaw, and traced its outline from her ear to the point of her chin. 'No, I won't lie to you,' he agreed. She turned her head and pressed her lips to his fingers, and with a little sound of satisfaction he leaned forward and took her mug before she dropped it.

He was going to kiss her again. She swallowed, and her eyes fluttered shut. The suspense was unbearable…

He shifted his weight, and she felt the hard length of his thigh against hers. One hand cupped her shoulder, the other curved around her cheek, cradling her head as his lips descended and brushed hers just lightly.

She whimpered and moved closer, reaching up to him,

and his arms slid round her, lifting her against him. 'You feel so good,' he murmured gruffly. He kissed her eyes, her cheeks, her chin, the tip of her nose—light, feathery kisses that teased and tormented and drove her crazy so that when his lips finally closed over hers she gave a little cry of relief and returned his kiss with feverish intensity.

One hand slid round and closed possessively over her hip, shifting her nearer him, and she squirmed closer. It wasn't enough. She needed to be closer still, much closer. Her fingers threaded through his hair, sifting the texture, loving the soft, silky feel of it against her fingertips.

His lips moved down her throat, pushing the soft fabric of her blouse aside, and he dispensed with the buttons and slid his hand round to cup her breast. Her bra was in the way. He muttered something and it was gone, unclipped and disposed of, pushed aside to give him access to his prize.

He didn't take it straight away, though. His tongue moved over the nipple, teasing it, and he blew softly across it so it pebbled even harder in the cool air. She arched, crying out his name, and his lips closed over it, drawing it in, suckling deeply.

How could it be so different? The last touch she had felt there had been her baby's, the soft, hungry rosebud mouth suckling greedily as Laura had lain in the curve of her mother's arm. This man's touch, with his rough stubble and skilful tongue that wrapped her nipple and drew it deep into his mouth, was light-years from the innocent suckling of a child. This was fierce and elemental and made her cry out, sobbing with the strength of emotion he aroused in her.

His touch gentled, his tongue soothing now, his lips soft against her delicate skin where his beard had scraped. He lifted his head and met her eyes, and she saw the question in the storm-grey depths.

'I want you,' he said softly. 'I'm not trying to rush you, but I want you to know how I feel.'

She closed her eyes. He was giving her a way out. Did she want to take it?

The phone rang, sounding far away, and with a muffled curse he rose and went over to it, his face taut.

'Latimer…Oh, hi, Rebecca. Yes, she's here. I'll get her.'

He held out the phone to Jo. 'Your mother.'

She stood, tugging her blouse closed across her aching breasts, and took the phone from him. 'Mum? What is it?'

'I'm sorry to interrupt, darling, but Laura's not very well. I think she might have flu. She's been sick, and she's got a temperature and a sore throat.'

'I'll be right home,' Jo promised, and hung up. Turning to Ed, she said, 'Laura's got flu. I have to go.'

He nodded. 'Perhaps it's just as well.' He nudged her hands aside and refastened her bra, then buttoned her blouse, before kissing her again softly on the mouth.

'The offer's open, remember. I'm not going anywhere, and I won't turn you away—any time, day or night. You're always welcome, whatever you come for. Don't feel if you come back we have to make love. We don't. Only if you want to.'

She did want to, that was the trouble. She wanted to so badly she could hardly force herself to walk out on him, but Laura was sick and Laura had to come first.

Perhaps it was just as well to remember it.

Laura's flu lasted three days, and left her with a hacking cough and no appetite. Jo, fortunately, didn't catch it, but she felt guilty, going to work and leaving Laura with her mother. She'd done it before, but for some reason—maybe because of Maurice—she was beginning to worry that she took her mother's help for granted.

She also felt guilty about being with Ed and fooling around while Laura needed her, and so she kept away from him.

Not that it was difficult. She was so busy it was ridiculous. She saw Mel at one of her antenatal clinics, although she'd finished the course of parentcraft and relaxation classes. Mel still had five weeks to go before the baby was due, and Jo was relieved to see that she was healthy and that everything was proceeding normally.

She didn't fancy trying to convince Mel that things were not straightforward enough to allow a home delivery. She had a feeling the woman would simply think that it was a ruse to get her to deliver in hospital, but fortunately it wasn't an issue.

The baby was the right size, the scan dates were spot on, the presentation was textbook perfect. Jo found the baby's heartbeat with the Sonicaid, and they listened to the steady, rapid rhythm as it was amplified by the little device.

'Oh, wow,' Mel said with a grin. 'It's so nice to hear it. It wriggles about all the time, but just to hear its heart—it makes it seem more alive—more real.'

Jo laughed. 'Oh, it's real. You wait a few weeks and you'll fine out just how real!'

'I know. Sioux—that's the girl down the track, you met her that time you came over—she's brought her baby up sometimes if Mick's been out, and she's cute but she's very, well, there! You can't forget her!'

'How are your neighbours?' she asked as Mel straightened her clothes.

'Well, Sioux's all right, but Mick's a bit scary. He's

got form, I think—not a nice man. Andy says we'll move on once the baby's come.'

Jo nodded. She'd spoken to the social services liaison officer, and yes, Mick did have a prison record, having caused grievous bodily harm to some poor innocent householder from whom he'd been trying to thieve. He'd also been convicted of dealing drugs. Not the sort of neighbours you would want in such isolated surroundings, particularly not with a baby around.

Jo knew it was none of her business, really, but Sioux's baby worried her. 'Mel,' she said carefully, 'does he hit her?'

Mel looked worried. 'I don't like to interfere. It's nothing to do with me.'

'No. I can understand that. I just thought I saw bruises on her face, and the baby's hand looked a little yellow, as if it might have been bruised at some time.'

Mel's eyes were downcast. 'I couldn't say,' she told Jo a little nervously. 'I try not to notice—it's none of my business. I just want to stay out of his way.'

Jo nodded. 'Yes. It sounds like a good idea. I expect the liaison officer knows.'

'Probably. He's been around a few times, but if Sioux won't say anything he can't do anything about it, can he? I think she's scared. I would be. I think she'd like to leave him, really, but he won't let her out of his sight.'

She stood and edged towards the door. 'I have to go— Andy's waiting. Look, you won't say anything, will you? If it got back to Mick that I'd said anything about it—'

'Anything about what? Didn't you know I'm deaf?'

Mel smiled gratefully. 'Cheers, Jo.'

'Take care. See you next week.'

She watched the woman go, and sighed, then picked up the phone. She needed to speak to Joe Saunders, the liaison officer, about Sioux and Mick and the baby. She'd spoken to him once, but she was more worried than ever about the baby now.

He was busy so she passed the case on to the health visitor as the baby was technically in her care. Hopefully something would be done before it was too late.

She looked at her watch. It was Tuesday afternoon, and she had calls to make after she'd finished her clinic. The final dress rehearsal for the pantomime was tonight, and then tomorrow they had a night off before the first performance on Thursday evening.

There were to be four performances—Thursday, Friday and Saturday evenings and a matinée on Saturday afternoon. The tickets were already sold out, and she just hoped everything would come together in time. Roz was getting a little panicky, but she usually did at this stage.

Still, tonight would be the acid test. If they got through it without a hitch it would be a miracle!

Ed stood backstage and watched Barry, the groom, flirting with Belle. His Belle. Once again, he'd hardly seen her for a week, and now here she was standing there while Barry made sheep's eyes at her.

Which would have been fine if they hadn't had such cameraderie off-stage as well!

Ed recognised his jealousy for the feeble thing it was, but it didn't stop him feeling it. The Beast was no better, smiling and teasing Jo and then getting to hold her in his arms on the stage and dance with her.

Ed wanted to dance with her, but not here, like this, in front of an audience. He wanted to dance with her somewhere private, where he could hold her close and be alone with her.

The audience seemed to be loving it, though. They laughed and clapped and cheered and roared and stamped and took part in all the usual 'Oh, no, he isn't' and 'Oh, yes, he is' banter that made pantomime what it was, and to everyone's amazement they fumbled their way through with only a few prompts.

It was the second night, and they were halfway through the run. Only two more performances, two more gatherings of this diverse collection of people, and it would all be over.

Ed knew from experience that there would be a flat spot afterwards, a strange emptiness on Wednesday nights at a quarter to eight. Before that, of course, there would be the adrenaline high of the final performance. There was a party planned for after they'd cleared the hall and packed up, and everyone was bringing something to eat and drink.

Knowing this lot, he thought as he prepared to go on for the finale, there would be a hell of a party.

He and the other villagers went on to the usual applause, and he took his place at the back of the stage and sang the penultimate number as the rest of the cast came on in pairs for the walkdown.

As Belle and the Beast were due to come on, there was a thud behind him and a sound like a pistol shot. He looked round, and Peter, the Beast, was standing on one leg, gasping with pain.

'Are you all right?' Jo was asking worriedly across the back of the stage.

'I'll be fine,' he whispered loudly. He limped on, and came down the stage, leaning heavily on Belle.

The final scene was mercifully short, and how Peter got through it Ed would never know, but as the curtain closed he sank down to the floor and grasped his ankle.

Ed was beside him in a moment. 'What happened?' he asked.

'I fell off the stage.'

'I heard.'

'I think the damn thing's broken.'

'I would say so. Let's move you.'

The groom, the back of the pantomime horse and Ed lifted Peter and carried him through to the dressing room, then set him down on top of the carpet bowls chest.

'What's happened?' Roz asked, squeezing through the crowd.

'He's broken his ankle. He needs to go to A and E. We can strap him up in Casualty at the hospital first, before the journey, but we can't do anything more with it here because the radiographer's not in till Monday.'

'Broken?' Roz said, horrified. 'Are you sure?'

'Certain,' Ed said. He'd got the shoe off by then and was looking at the ankle, and it wasn't good. Unless he was mistaken it would need plating.

'Will I be able to do tomorrow's performances?' Peter asked worriedly.

'No.'

'But I have to!'

'The show must go on? Certainly, but not with you, my friend. You'll still be in hospital. You've broken your fibula.'

Jo appeared at his side. 'I hate to add to the stress,' she said quietly, 'but whoever plays the Beast tomorrow will need those breeches, and if they go to A and E with him they'll cut them off.'

'They can't cut them off, they're hired!' Anne said, panic-stricken.

'Take them off,' Peter said. 'Quick, before the feeling comes back too much.'

So they did, there in the dressing room, carefully wiggling the trousers off his uninjured leg first before supporting the bad one and easing the second trouser leg down and over the foot.

By the time they'd finished Peter was grey and sweating, but the breeches were intact.

'Brilliant. Well done. Now all we have to do is work out who's going to be wearing them tomorrow,' Roz said, looking round. 'It needs to be someone with a minor part, but who knows the play well enough to learn Peter's lines and moves by two-thirty tomorrow—someone of about the same size.'

Ed was bending over Peter's foot, winding a scarf around it as a makeshift support so they could take him to the hospital. He heard the room go quiet and, glancing over his shoulder, he saw they were all looking at him.

'What?' he said. 'What is it?'

'Can you roar?'

His eyes widened. 'Oh, no. Oh, no, Roz, I can't! You can't do this to me! No! Absolutely not! I refuse!'

Laura was right, Jo thought, Ed made a wonderful Beast. He could sing, he could dance, he had stage presence— and he didn't tread on her toes once.

He'd fluffed his lines in the afternoon performance, but not so badly that anyone had noticed, and the rest of them had all picked up and carried on regardless. The Saturday night performance was the one to worry about, she thought, because he was likely to be put off by all the audience participation and last-night mayhem.

She just hoped nobody did anything nasty to him to make him corpse.

Ed's first scene was when Belle's father picked the rose, and he entered with a mighty roar that brought a howl of laughter from the audience.

Oh, dear, it's going to be like that, she thought, but he waited, gave them time to laugh and continued like a pro. He'd done it before, of course, but not for years. He must just be a natural, she thought, and wondered if he realised he'd be in it for life now.

The audience were quieter for the first meeting between Belle and the Beast, and as they stood close together she could feel the tension in him.

He's got stage fright, Jo thought, and wondered if he'd get through it, but there was no trace of nerves in his voice.

'Are you frightened of me, Belle?' he said.

'No, I'm not frightened.'

'And do you like my magnificent castle?'

He gestured at the amateur stage flats, the hand-painted interior of the 'castle', and somehow she stopped the smile that always rose to her lips at that point. 'Yes, it's very—magnificent,' she said, deadpan.

'Good. Then you will stay for ever!' He held out his hand, grey-gloved, with cardboard talons taped on the ends of his fingers. 'Dance with me,' he ordered.

She stepped back a fraction. 'Haven't you forgotten something?'

'Dance with me *now*!'

'No,' she said firmly. 'A gentleman should be good mannered towards a lady. Will you dance with me, *please*?'

He held out his hand again and paused, as if chastened. 'Will you dance with me—*please*?' he said humbly.

A shiver of awareness ran down her spine. 'I should be honoured,' she replied, and curtseyed deeply.

The audience aahed, the music of *Beauty and the Beast* started, and she moved into his arms. Immediately the audience receded, and it was just the two of them, alone, moving in harmony as they circled the stage in a slow waltz.

His hand lay lightly over the small of her back, guiding her, and she could feel the imprint of it against her skin long after the scene was over.

It wasn't only his touch, either. In the next scene, after the interval, there was something in his voice. She couldn't see his face because the mask came down too low, but when the Beast asked Belle if there was someone in her former life, someone she might have married, there was more than just the script involved.

'Oh, no,' she replied, 'I shall have to fall in love before I marry.'

'And how will you know when you've fallen in love?' he asked, and she could have sworn he was asking her, not Belle.

She wished she could see his eyes. 'I don't know, it hasn't happened yet,' she replied, and he hung his head in a gesture that made her want to comfort him. The audience felt it too, and sighed softly. 'But I'm sure I'll know when it does,' she added, and it was for him, not the Beast, that she said the words.

The next time they were on stage together was the last scene, and it was one Jo hated doing. That afternoon Ed had been struggling with his lines, but now he seemed word perfect, and because she didn't have to worry about him her concentration was on the scene itself.

In the scene she arrived back at the Beast's castle just as he was dying, and had to throw herself, weeping, beside him. In fact, it was Peter's wife, dressed as the Beast in the mask and lying behind some bushes, but it was Ed she spoke to, and Ed's voice that told her he loved her.

'Oh, Beast,' she sobbed, 'don't die! I love you too. Can you hear me, Beast? *I love you*!'

The lights dimmed and the scene changed to spring.

As the lights came up, Ed, dressed now as a handsome prince, walked downstage towards her.

His eyes locked with hers, and she didn't dare believe the look in them. Had those words of love really been for her?

The audience was laughing and catcalling the so-called 'Prince', the girls were wolf-whistling at him, but she ignored them, transfixed by the look in his eyes.

'Don't you know me, Belle?' he ad-libbed at last, and she realised she'd fluffed her lines.

'Who are you?' she said hastily. 'Where is my Beast?'

His mouth quirked, his eyes gleamed with approval and he went on, 'I am a Prince. You see me as I once was, before an evil spell transformed me into the Beast. Now the spell has been broken, thanks to you, Belle.'

'But how?' she asked.

'By loving me,' he replied, and the look in his eyes intensified.

The scene moved on to the end, carrying her in a daze, and then the Prince held out his hand. 'Marry me, Belle,' he commanded.

She smiled, her heart thumping in her chest, and groped for her lines. 'Haven't you forgotten something?'

'Marry me *now*?' His face quirked in a smile, and then it faded. 'Will you marry me...please?' he asked sincerely.

'I should be honoured,' she replied. At least, she would have done, but her voice stuck and she lost the words. Tears filled her eyes, and she felt absurd, but the rest of the cast then became involved in a bit of silliness, and she had a moment to compose herself before the end of the scene. The curtains closed for the ten-second change into her wedding dress, and she was all fingers and thumbs.

Was it true? Did Ed love her, or was he just acting? Had he really just proposed?

He appeared behind her when she was standing in her underwear, and leaned forward, his mouth by her ear. 'Do you have any idea how fetching you are in those net curtains?' he murmured, and she spluttered and tugged the wedding dress on.

'Just zip me up and don't be cheeky,' she said, and someone elbowed him out of the way, scooped her hair up into a bun and jammed the tiara on her head.

Then came the walkdown to the finale, and in the tumult of the applause a huge bouquet of flowers appeared in her arms, just as they launched into the final chorus. She nudged Barry. 'What do I do with these?' she said through a smile that wouldn't be controlled.

'Pass them back,' he said, and she handed them behind her and joined in.

The audience wouldn't let them go, calling them back again and again, and in the end they just closed the curtain and went off. The applause continued even after the house lights came on, and backstage it was a scene of utter chaos and delirium.

Everyone was clapping Ed on the back and telling him he was fantastic, but Jo just wanted to get changed and get out of there. Something had happened between them tonight, something magical, and she wanted to be alone with him and talk about it.

'Mum, you were brilliant,' Laura said, hugging her, and then she turned to Ed, standing there in his breeches with his shirt hanging open, and hugged him too. 'Told you you'd do the Beast well,' she said smugly, and vanished to change.

Jo was trying not to look at him. He was altogether too enticing dressed like that, and she didn't want to embarrass either of them by staring at him. She went behind the costume rail that doubled as a screen, peeled off the dreaded net curtains and tugged on her jeans and sweatshirt, then assembled her costumes and took them out to Anne.

'Here,' she said. 'Do you want me to do anything with them?'

'No, that's fine. Thanks. You were marvellous—and isn't Ed a find?'

Jo smiled. 'Isn't he?' She left Anne and went to help clear up. The quicker it was done the quicker they could be alone—and the quicker she would have her answers.

The party was a riot, but Jo's heart wasn't in it. There was food, and music, and they were all congratulating Ed and thanking him for stepping in. Then he managed to escape from them all and grabbed Jo, towing her into a space.

'Dance with me,' he said.

She laughed. 'Haven't you forgotten something?'

'Dance with me *now*?'

She laughed again. 'Some people never learn,' she said, and went into his arms. This time he held her close, and the heat flared between them in seconds.

'Come to me tonight,' he murmured. 'Please?'

She met his eyes and her heart jerked against her ribs.

'Yes,' she said simply.

CHAPTER EIGHT

ED WAS waiting for her. The door opened as Jo went down the path, and he drew her into his arms and kissed her gently.

'I thought you'd changed your mind.'

'No—I had a shower. I was all greasepaint and hot lights.'

He smiled briefly. 'Ditto.'

She touched his hair, and it was still damp, roughly towelled. A tiny rivulet ran down into his collar, and she followed its path with her fingertip. 'You're dripping,' she told him.

'I was in a hurry.' He looked away, then looked back, his eyes alight with a strange intensity. 'Dance with me?' he said with a little smile. The music was soft and romantic, a compilation love album that went from one slow and dreamy number to another.

She'd thought their loving would be hurried, but Ed seemed in no hurry at all. He held her close against his chest, one hand on her back, the other holding her hand folded against his shoulder, and he swayed slowly in time to the music, letting it wash over them, letting the mood carry them.

Finally, his control seemed to snap, and he stopped and looked down into her eyes. 'Make love with me, Jo,' he said, and his voice was gruff and low and unsteady.

A tremor ran through her. She reached up on tiptoe and kissed him in answer, and he scooped her up into his arms and carried her up to the bedroom. The lights were low, the quilt turned back in readiness, and he undressed her without preamble, stripping off his own clothes before turning back to her.

She felt almost sick with anticipation. It had been so long, and she had crushed any feelings so ruthlessly that she wasn't sure what to expect. She just knew there was no going back.

Ed held out his hand and drew her to the bed, then lay beside her, propping himself on one elbow so he was facing her. Jo lay on her back, her eyes fixed on his, wishing it was over, wishing he would do something—

'I love you,' he said softly.

Her eyes filled with tears. 'Oh, Ed,' she whispered, and reached for him.

He was tender and generous. He didn't hurry her, despite the fact that he was shaking with the effort of holding himself back, and when she splintered in his arms, only then did he let himself go, crying out her name as his body stiffened in her arms.

His chest heaved, his breathing harsh and ragged, and he shifted his weight so that he lay half beside her, his head on her shoulder, one hand lying possessively over her breast while he waited for his heart to slow.

The air was cool, and after a while he moved, pulling the quilt over them. 'Are you OK?'

She laughed a little unsteadily. 'I think so. I'm not sure—I don't feel as if I've quite come back down to earth yet.'

He chuckled. 'I know the feeling.' He kissed her lightly, brushing the hair from her eyes. 'You're so beautiful,' he murmured, and for the first time she dared to believe him.

She tunnelled her fingers through his hair. 'So are you.' She ran her hand over the smooth skin of his shoulder, feeling the hard muscle of his arm under her palm. 'I just want to touch you—you feel so good.'

He groaned softly as she slid her hand down and over his hip. 'I want you again,' he murmured.

His mouth brushed hers, and unbelievably she felt the renewed stirrings of desire. This time he was more re- laxed, lazier and even less hurried, and by the time they drifted back to earth the second time she was almost asleep.

'I have to go home,' she mumbled sleepily. 'Laura doesn't know where I am.'

'Isn't that just as well?'

She felt her responsibilities pulling at her. 'Probably.' There were other responsibilities preying on her mind as well—or perhaps, more accurately, irresponsibilities.

'Ed, I don't want to put a damper on things,' she said, 'but do you think it would be an idea if you wrote me out a prescription for the morning-after pill? I don't re- call us doing anything about it, and I've already had one unplanned pregnancy.'

His eyes were shadowed. 'Don't worry,' he said qui- etly. 'I can't get you pregnant, Jo. I'm sterile.'

'Sterile?'

The shock froze her for a moment, then compassion rose in her and she reached for him.

'Oh, Ed—I'm sorry.' No wonder he'd looked sad when all the babies were born!

'It's all right, Jo,' he murmured, hugging her. 'I'm fine. I knew it was going to happen so I had time to do something about it. I can have children, just not like this.'

She looked at him, then wriggled out of his arms and sat up against the pillows, hugging her arms around her. 'What do you mean?' she asked. 'How did you know?'

He shifted so that he was beside her, and pulled up

the quilt. 'I had testicular cancer when I was twenty,' he told her in a matter-of-fact voice. 'I found it early, they removed the affected testicle and gave me chemotherapy which knocked out the sperm-producing cells in the other one, but not until I'd had the chance to have some frozen, just in case.'

'And are you OK?' she asked, far more worried about the threat to his life than the fact that he couldn't have children. 'Are you clear?'

'Oh, yes, I've been clear for years,' he assured her, and the tension left her.

'I didn't notice,' she said with a strained laugh. 'Just shows how much attention I was paying.'

'You wouldn't be able to tell. They put in an implant so, as far as anyone's concerned, I'm no different. I just—fire blanks.' He gave a wry grin, and she took his hand and squeezed it.

'Oh, Ed, I'm sorry. Why didn't you tell me?'

He looked away. 'I just—I don't know. Selfish reasons, really. In the past it's put people off. They—um—they don't seem to think they want to get involved. I don't know if they feel there's still a threat, or if they feel they could catch cancer from me, or if they feel I'm less of a man—'

'But that's nonsense!' she protested.

'I know,' he said heavily, 'but it's the way it is. I just didn't want you walking away from me too. Somehow I knew that would hurt far more than anything else had ever done, and I didn't dare risk it.' He squeezed her hand. 'I'm sorry. I should have told you.'

'Oh, Ed. I wouldn't walk away from you!' she whispered unsteadily. 'I don't think I could!'

His arm came round her and he hugged her close. 'Oh, Jo...' His voice was choked, and she slid her arms round him and hugged him tight.

Words seemed unnecessary. Instead they merely lay there, wrapped in each other's arms, just enjoying being close. The CD player had come to a halt, and the house was quiet. Outside a gate creaked, and then running foot-steps sounded in the garden.

'Who's that?' Ed said, lifting his head, a frown creas-ing his brow.

'I don't know—have a look.'

He turned out the light and went to the window, just as there was a knock on the back door.

'I can't see. I'll go down. Stay here.'

He pulled on his clothes and ran down the stairs, and Jo dressed herself more carefully and crept to the top of the stairs. Then she froze. There was no way she could go downstairs because their visitor was Laura!

'Laura? What's wrong?'

'Can I come in?'

He opened the door to the tearful girl. 'Of course you can come in. What's the matter?'

'I just need to talk to someone, and Mum's out. I saw your lights on—I hope you don't mind?'

'No, of course not. Come and sit down—do you want a cup of tea?'

She shook her head. 'No. I just wanted to talk to you…' Without warning, she threw herself into his arms and sobbed her heart out.

'Laura,' he said gently, and led her to the settee. Where's Jo? he thought. She ought to be here. God alone knows what's wrong.

He let Laura cry for a while, then handed her a clump of tissues and waited while she mopped herself up. 'OK, let's have it. What's upset you? You seemed OK earlier. Has something happened?'

'Grannie…'

'What about Grannie?' he asked, concerned. 'Is she ill?'

Laura shook her head. 'No. She's fine. Dr Parker came round—they were at the panto and they came back to the house afterwards. I came back with Mum after the party and went to bed, but I couldn't sleep. I got up and went down to get a drink, and we didn't have anything much in our fridge so I went into Grannie's kitchen— well, I *was* going into Grannie's kitchen.'

'And?' he prompted.

'Grannie was there with Dr Parker. I was going to go in, but then he said something…'

'What did he say?' Ed asked when it was obvious she wasn't going to go on.

She sniffed. 'He said…she was very beautiful, and he loved her. He said he wanted to marry her. He told her to think about it.' She twisted her hands together. 'Then he kissed her goodbye—properly, you know. Not just a peck on the cheek, but a real kiss.'

'I see.'

'He shouldn't have done,' Laura said emphatically. 'She's Grandad's wife. It didn't seem right.'

'But they're both alone now, Laura. Maybe they're lonely.'

'They still shouldn't do *that*!'

Ed sighed inwardly. 'People do, you know. I know it can be hard to accept, but when you're in love there usually is a strong physical element—'

'But not *Grannie*!' she said, and burst into tears again. 'She's going to marry him, and then what will happen? She'll move out, and Mummy will be out at night, like she is tonight, and I'll be all on my own.'

'Does it frighten you, being on your own?'

'No. I just hate it, and I hate change, and everything's going to change, and I like it like it is…'

She curled up in the corner, sobbing into the tissues. Ed looked up and saw Jo, hovering in the doorway at the bottom of the stairs. He shook his head, and she moved back out of sight, her face tormented.

'Let's go in the kitchen and fix a drink,' he said clearly, and put his arm round Laura's shoulder. 'I think I've got some cola—do you fancy a glass? I might have some chocolate biscuits as well.'

She sniffed and nodded, and he led her out of the sitting room. Please, God, Jo, use your common sense, he prayed, and out of the corner of his eye he saw her slip across the room. Then there was a knocking on the door, and it opened and Jo called out.

'Ed? I don't suppose you know where Laura is, do you? She's not at home.'

Thank you, God, he mouthed, and stuck his head round the door and winked at her. 'She's here. She was a bit upset, so she came for a chat.'

Jo walked into the kitchen, took one look at her daughter and held out her arms. 'Oh, sweetheart, what's the matter?'

'I missed you, you weren't there,' Laura mumbled from the depths of her mother's sweatshirt. 'And Grannie's going to marry Dr Parker.'

Jo patted her shoulder and met Ed's eyes over Laura's head. Her eyes were drenched with misery, and she bit her lip. 'Is she?' she said finally. 'I didn't know.'

'He asked her tonight.'

'And did she say yes?'

Laura shook her head. 'She didn't say anything, but I know she will.' She lifted her head. 'He kissed her, Mum. It was really tacky.'

'Tacky?' she said gently. 'Or just a bit unexpected? Did they know you were there?'

She shook her head. 'No, of course not, but I couldn't

get away without them seeing me. I had to sneak off when he was kissing her. I think I could have danced round them and they wouldn't have noticed. It was gross.'

'But they wouldn't have done it if they'd known you were there.'

'And that's better?'

Jo closed her eyes and hugged Laura again. 'I don't know. Come on, it's late. Time for bed.'

'Where were you?' she asked, and Laura met Ed's eyes in desperation.

'I had to visit someone,' she said, and he could tell from her eyes that she hated deceiving Laura. Now, though, was obviously not the time to tell the child the truth. 'Come on. Ed, thanks.'

He gave her a reassuring smile. 'My pleasure,' he said softly, and her eyes filled a little. He laid a hand on her shoulder and squeezed gently. 'I'll see you both in the morning.'

Jo nodded and took Laura out. He watched them go up the path in the moonlight, then locked the door with a heavy sigh.

Poor Laura, coming face to face with reality. It was a hard lesson to learn. Still, Jo would talk to her.

Ed went up to bed, and the sheets held the lingering traces of Jo's perfume, mixed with the warm, musky scent of their loving.

He lay down in the tangled sheets and breathed in her scent and wished that she was there.

'How is she?'

'Oh, mixed up. She's gone out with Cara—they're meeting some friends. She's hardly seen them, she's been so busy with the pantomime.'

They strolled along the seafront, their arms brushing.

Ed didn't hold her hand or put his arm round Jo, although he wanted to, but she seemed withdrawn. He shoved his hands in his pockets instead.

'Have you spoken to your mother?'

'Yes. She told me all about Maurice. She's worried about Laura. I didn't tell her what happened—I didn't want her to feel distressed, and I know she would. She's still thinking about his proposal, but she's got her sparkle back. It's odd, I never thought she would, but they seem to have given each other a new lease of life. They're both acting like spring chickens. I just wish Laura could be happy for them.'

'Mmm. I know what you mean. Maurice seems endlessly cheerful, and your mother certainly seems bright.'

'She's worried about Laura, though. She seems to think that if she marries Maurice and he retires, they'll be spending a lot of time away. That's what he's talking about, going on the holidays he'd planned to take when he retired, doing all the things he's always wanted to do. And that means, of course, that if she goes with him she won't be here for Laura.'

'That might not be such a problem,' he said carefully.

'Why?'

They reached a breakwater, and he drew her down to sit on it, looking out over the sea. He caught sight of a striped pebble, and he picked it up and turned it over in his hands, inspecting it while he cast about for words.

'Last night—being with you, loving you—was the best thing that's ever happened to me,' he told her quietly. 'I meant it when I said that I love you. I do, probably more than I can ever tell you. I want to spend my life with you, Jo. I want to marry you, and be with you for the rest of my life. If we can, I want us to have children, but if not it doesn't matter. You've got Laura, and I'd do everything I could to be a good father to her.'

He searched her eyes, and saw misery there in their lovely hazel depths. 'Oh, Ed, we can't,' she said heavily. 'Not now, anyway. Not with my mother getting married.'

'But it's ideal! We could work our nights off so that there was always someone there for Laura—'

'And be permanently exhausted because we had broken nights every night? Ed, it wouldn't work. It's not that I don't love you. I do. Last night proved that to me if nothing else could. You were wonderful with Laura.'

'So what's the problem?' he said. 'We can work it out, Jo.'

She shook her head. 'I just feel…it would be too much for her, with my mother as well. She's really very shocked about it. She wouldn't look at her this morning.'

He tried another tack. 'What will you do when your mother marries Maurice? Who will look after her when you're on call?'

She shrugged. 'I don't know, I haven't worked it out. I'll have to do something—get a lodger? Find an au pair? I don't know, I haven't had time to think. I just know this isn't right for her, not now.' She turned to him, and he could see the sadness in her eyes. 'I'm sorry, Ed. I can't—not now. Maybe later.'

He searched her face, then nodded. 'OK. You know her better than I do. We'll give her time to get used to the idea—but I'm not giving up, Jo. There's too much at stake, for both of us. I love you. I'm not going to stop loving you just because it isn't easy.'

She slipped her hand into his and squeezed it, and he returned the pressure reassuringly. 'Thanks,' she said softly. 'I knew you'd understand.'

He looked out across the waves, his heart impatient. He wanted to be with her now, to have the right to walk hand in hand with her, without anyone looking and commenting. He wanted to hold her at night, to make love to her, to have children with her.

He wanted it all and, because she was the woman she was, it wasn't possible.

Not yet, anyway.

Hopefully, Laura would come round in time.

'Have you ever said anything to Laura about us?' he asked curiously.

'No. Why?'

He shrugged. 'I just wondered. She might not react like you think.'

Jo shook her head. 'Ed, I can't risk it, not now. She's so shaken up about Mum I just daren't rock her boat any more.'

'So where do we go from here?' he asked, dreading her answer. 'Is that it? Do we stop seeing each other?'

Their eyes locked. 'I don't know,' she said miserably. 'I would just feel so awful if she caught us—last night could have been dreadful.'

'Maybe we need to go somewhere else. Perhaps I need to move.'

'That would just make it harder.'

'What do you suggest? We drive out into the forest and make love in the car? Jo, we're too old for that sort of thing. Knowing our luck, we'd get caught by the police.'

She gave a little laugh. 'Yes, very likely. Ed, I don't know the answer. Perhaps we just need to spend time together in front of her—come round for a meal, have coffee, play cards with her, watch a video—just be part of the family.'

'You don't think she'll feel she's in the way then? She must have friends with single parents who are having relationships—how do they cope? This happens all the time, Jo. It's not just us that has this problem.'

'I don't know.' She stood up. 'I need to go back. I've got things to do I've been putting off because of the panto—washing and tedious things like that.'

'Me, too. I'll come with you.'

They turned and headed back. The beach was almost deserted, just a few fishermen and someone walking a dog. It was peaceful and beautiful, and Ed wished things were different. He'd just proposed to Jo, and it should have been the happiest day of their lives.

Instead it was filled with uncertainty and confusion.

Damn.

He kicked a pebble, frustrated and disappointed and yet understanding, and Jo sighed.

'I'm sorry, Ed.'

'Don't be. You're doing what you have to do. I'll still be around. Maybe Laura needs to go out for sleep-overs occasionally.'

She laughed. 'I can't send her off to friends every night—she'd smell a rat!'

'Just every now and again. You've got rights as well, Jo. Don't forget that.'

He hugged her briefly, then released her and looked up. A fisherman up ahead was casting his line, and a young couple had wandered onto the beach behind him.

'That line's very close,' Ed said, just as there was a scream and the woman threw her hands up to her face. 'Whoops. I think he's hooked her. So much for my day off.' He headed across the beach at a run, with Jo after him, and arrived at the woman just as the fisherman did.

'Sorry, love, I didn't see you—are you all right?' he was saying.

'It hurts!' she wailed, and the man with her was hugging her and yelling at the fisherman.

'I'm a doctor,' Ed said, cutting through the pandemonium. 'Can I have a look?'

'It's my eyebrow,' she wailed. 'He's stuck it in my eyebrow!'

'Let me see,' Ed said firmly. Taking her hands, he lifted them away to reveal the hook firmly embedded in her left eyebrow, about two-thirds of the way along.

'Oh, hell, Tammy,' the man said, and turned away, gagging.

'Pull it out,' she said frantically, but the fisherman intervened.

'No, you can't, it's barbed. You'll have to take it— through—you need to cut the end off. Here.' He pulled some scissors out of his pocket and lifted them towards her face.

'Oh, no,' the man groaned. Running down to the water's edge, he lost his breakfast.

'Wimp,' the girl said scornfully as the fisherman snipped through the line, leaving the hook where it was. 'Bloody hell, it hurts worse than having my nose pierced. How are we going to get it out, then?'

'We'll have to do what he says,' Ed told her, 'but I'll take you down to Casualty and do it there. I'll give you a local anaesthetic first, and then we'll worry about it.'

'I'll come,' the fisherman said. 'I'll pack my gear up and follow you.'

'What about your friend?' Jo said to her.

She looked down the beach and shrugged. 'What about him? He'll come. Hey, Paddy, come on. We're going to the hospital.'

He walked reluctantly back to them, dragging his feet. Ed noticed he had rings and studs in his ears and nose and one eyebrow, anyway, so why the fish-hook should upset him so much he couldn't imagine.

'Do you want a lift, or have you got a car?' he asked.

'We'll come on the bike,' he said.

'Not like this, I'm not!' the girl protested. 'Can I come with you?'

Ed nodded. 'You coming?' he asked Jo. 'I might need a hand.'

She hesitated, then seemed to catch on and, to his relief, agreed. The last thing he wanted was to be alone in his car with a girl who later accused him of anything suspicious. With Jo there, it wouldn't happen.

They arrived at the hospital in convoy. Paddy followed them in at a distance and sat on the other side of the waiting room, shielding his eyes. 'Turns me right up,' he confessed, and picked up a magazine.

'Lot of use you are,' Tammy grumbled, and went through with them to a cubicle, leaving the fisherman to keep Paddy company.

Ed asked her to lie down, then injected the area with local anaesthetic. Once it had taken effect he asked Jo to hold the hook steady while he snipped off the end with some cutters and pushed it through.

The end of the barb came out through the top of her eyebrow, and Ed showed it to her. He washed the area well and, using a syringe, he squirted saline through the puncture wound to flush it. 'You'll need antibiotics,' he told her. 'I'll give you a prescription, but you must take them, otherwise you could get a nasty infection.'

'OK.'

He stood back. 'There you go, then. All done.'

She stood up, grinned and thanked them, then disappeared into the Ladies. A few moments later she reappeared and called Paddy.

'Hey, cool!' he said with a laugh.

Ed and Jo looked up, and Ed blinked. 'Am I seeing things?' he asked.

Jo chuckled. 'I don't think so.'

Tammy met their eyes and grinned. 'Seemed a shame

to waste it,' she said. As she turned to go out the sun glinted on the sleeper that was now threaded through her eyebrow.

'Cheers, mate,' she said to the fisherman, and followed Paddy through the door.

The fisherman turned to them and shrugged. 'Takes all sorts,' he said with a grin. 'Think I might go home now. Wait till I tell the missis what I caught for dinner!'

Ed laughed and waved, and turned to Jo. 'Back to our chores?'

'We should.'

'Thanks for coming down with me. I didn't fancy getting stuck with a sexual harassment claim if she'd decided to get rich quick. It's been done.'

'I don't think she would have done, but she might have propositioned you.'

He laughed. 'In which case, even more thanks. I've seen some strange things in my time, but that just takes the biscuit. Anyone who can do that to themselves is too kinky for me.'

He drove Jo home, parking outside the front of his house. 'I don't suppose I can entice you in?'

She smiled. 'Better not. Laura might come back.'

'OK.' He leaned on the car roof, and looked into her eyes. 'I love you,' he murmured.

'I love you too, Ed. I'm sorry.'

'Don't be sorry. We'll work things out.'

He watched her go, and wondered if he was just being a dreamer or if there really was a chance for them.

So near, and yet so far…

CHAPTER NINE

'MUM, can I stay with Lucy? Her brother's going away for the weekend and she's allowed a friend. Can I go?'

'Sure,' Jo said with a smile, and wondered if her daughter could read the guilty delight in her eyes. A whole weekend? And, furthermore, they weren't on call!

She had to stop herself running down the path to tell Ed. The last ten days had been hell, trying to snatch moments alone, worrying about Laura, trying to convince her mother to take the happiness Maurice was offering and not feel guilty about it—and now here was the weekend on a plate!

She told Ed the next morning instead, and he smiled for the rest of the day. Jo did, too, wandering round humming and chatting to everyone, and it made her realise how dismal she'd been feeling.

Then, as luck would have it, Lucy's mother became ill with tonsillitis, and the whole plan was cancelled.

'Can she come here?' Laura asked on Friday night, miserable at the thought of her spoilt weekend.

Jo, whose weekend had been ruined anyway, agreed, and rang Ed. 'I'm sorry, we're going to have to cancel,' she told him in a hushed voice. 'Lucy's mother's ill so Lucy's coming here.'

'Ah. Well, why don't we do what you suggested some time ago, and I'll come to you? I've bought food—why don't I come round and cook it for you there, and they can make pizza or whatever and watch telly, and we can sit in the kitchen and chat.'

'It's not the same,' she said, disappointment in her voice.

'No, but I'd rather be with you and the girls than without you.'

'Really?'

'Of course really. I'm well aware of what being the parent of a teenager involves—my older sister's got three. I'll come round soon—six-thirty? Then you can chat to me while I cook.'

'Thanks,' she said softly. 'You are kind. I'm sorry.'

'I just love you. See you soon.'

She cradled the phone thoughtfully. He did love her, she realised, quite genuinely. He'd been very patient. Perhaps he was right—they ought to start getting Laura used to his presence in her life.

She went out of the kitchen and found Laura sprawled on her stomach in front of the television, eating crisps. 'Ring Lucy. She can come here. I'll fetch her as soon as she's ready.'

'Really? Thanks, Mum, that's magic!'

She leapt to her feet, gave Jo a flying hug and ran to the phone.

'That was wonderful. You are the best cook.'

He chuckled. 'You can wash up.'

'No problem. I'll stick it in the sink now to soak. I don't suppose you want to make the coffee while I do that?'

'Some people will use any excuse to get out of a chore,' he teased, but he made the coffee anyway while she cleared up the kitchen. Then, like a magician pulling a rabbit out of a hat, he produced a box of chocolates and put them on the table. '*Voilà*,' he said with a grin.

'Oh, wow, chocs!' Laura said, wandering into the kitchen. 'Are they for us?'

'Us, you and Lucy, or us, all of us?' Ed asked, smiling.

'Oh. Are they yours?'

'No, they're ours,' he told her. 'Open them and help yourselves—if you're allowed?'

'Mum?'

Jo nodded. 'Don't eat them all. You can have two each.'

'Bags the hazelnut whirl,' Lucy said, and they dived into the box.

Ed met Jo's eyes across their heads, and he winked. The girls went off with brimming glasses of fizzy drinks and their hoard of chocolates, and disappeared back into the sitting room.

'I bet they've taken my favourites,' Ed grumbled good-naturedly, fishing through the chocolates.

'Serve you right for being so generous. I would have told them to take a hike,' she said with a chuckle. 'I'll be all right, I like the coconut ones.'

They drank their coffee at the kitchen table, and after a while Ed leant back in his chair and said, 'Would they mind if you came back with me for a bit? Half an hour or so? They seem happy enough, your mother's in—how about it? No strings, just another cup of coffee and a hug?'

'Sounds wonderful,' Jo said, and wished she dared to make it longer. She stuck her head round the door. 'I'm going to help Ed take the dishes and things back to the cottage, and have a coffee. I'll be about half an hour, OK? Grannie's here if you want her.'

'OK,' Laura said, not bothering to turn her head, and Jo wondered if Laura actually minded or if she herself was being too fussy.

'All right?' Ed said as she went back to the kitchen.

'Fine.'

They picked up all the dishes and the rest of the chocolates, and went across the gardens to Ed's. It was so close it was silly to worry, especially as they could see the house from the cottage, but Jo still felt a little pang of guilt.

Ed, predictably, noticed. 'Stop it,' he said gently. 'You're allowed a life.'

'Am I?'

'Yes,' he said firmly. Taking the dishes from her, he put them down in the kitchen, put the kettle on and lit the fire. It wasn't cold as the central heating was on still, but it made the place cheery. He found a CD—classical this time, moody but not seductive—put it on and dropped into the corner of the settee beside her with a grin.

'Alone at last,' he said in a theatrical tone, and she laughed.

'Yes, but not for long,' she told him. 'A quick cup of coffee, that's all.'

'And a hug,' he reminded her. 'Don't forget the hug.'

She smiled and wriggled over into his arms. 'One hug coming up,' she said, and his arms wrapped round her and drew her closer. They sat in silence for a while, listening to the music and just being together, then he tipped his head and looked at her. 'OK?'

'Mmm. You're very comfy to rest on. I wish I could stay here for ever.'

'So do I.' He sighed and buried his lips in her hair. 'I miss you so much,' he told her. 'I know it's silly—we see each other all the time, but it's not the same as being alone.'

'You just want to have your evil way with me,' she teased.

'I do, you're quite right, but there's much more to it

than that and you know it,' he said quietly. 'Still, I'll wait. Our time will come.'

'It'll go as well,' she said regretfully, easing out of his arms. 'I have to go.'

'Already? We haven't had coffee.'

'No time. I don't want to cause problems—you know how Laura's feeling.'

Ed stood up and pulled Jo to her feet, then drew her into his arms. 'I know. How about a goodnight kiss— are you allowed that?'

'Ooh, a little one,' she said with a smile, and he chuckled, then lowered his mouth to hers.

It was meant to be short and sweet. In the end it was white-hot, passionate and stopped only because they needed to breathe. Ed sagged against the door, pulling her with him, and laughed weakly. 'You'll be the death of me,' he muttered into her hair, and hugged her. 'Go on, go home while I'll still let you, or you won't be back before midnight.'

She went up on tiptoe, dropped a kiss on his cheek and moved him away from the door. He followed her, standing on the step and watching her. It made her feel safe somehow, knowing he was looking out for her as she went home. Not that it was dangerous, exactly, in Yoxburgh. It was the fact that he cared enough to do it.

She turned at the gate and waved, and he lifted a hand. She was very tempted to go back, but she didn't. She turned away, closed the gate and went back to the girls. As she let herself in through the back door, she heard them talking in the kitchen.

They hadn't heard her come in, and Lucy was talking about Ed.

'It was nice of him to bring the chocolates—did you see that meal he cooked your mum? He must really fancy her.'

'Don't be daft,' Laura replied. 'They just work to-gether.'

Lucy giggled. 'Don't be daft yourself. Didn't you see the way he looked at her? I reckon they're having an affair.'

'What?' Laura sounded shocked, and Jo rolled her eyes and inched back against the door, out of sight. 'Of course they're not!'

'Why not? My mum's having an affair with her boy-friend—they think I don't know, but I do. It's quite sweet, really. He's nuts about her. He looks at her like Ed looks at your mum, and she's potty about him. I think they'll get married soon, but I expect Mum wants to be sure first. She doesn't want another messy divorce.'

Jo decided she'd heard enough. She opened the door noisily, banged it shut and called out, 'Hi, girls, I'm back— Oh, there you are. Everything OK?'

Laura looked searchingly at her. 'Yeah, fine. You weren't very long.'

'I said I wouldn't be,' she reminded Laura, and could have kicked herself for not staying longer, although on second thoughts that might not have been such a good idea. The way their conversation had been going, the girls would have had them married off.

Oh, what a wonderful thought. Perhaps she should have been longer—given Lucy time to work on Laura.

'Right, girls, bedtime,' she said firmly, and chivvied them up the stairs.

On Tuesday night Jo was on call, and after she'd re-turned from a visit she parked the car in the alleyway beside the house instead of on the drive, and went in to see Ed. It was ten-thirty. He was in the shower and he answered the door in a towel, gave her a slightly damp kiss and told her to put the kettle on.

'I'd rather join you in the shower,' she said, and after a second a grin broke out on his face.

'Last one in's a chicken,' he said, and ran upstairs, with Jo in hot pursuit.

After their shower, and the inevitable sequel, they lay in his bed, wrapped in each other's arms and enjoying just being together.

'I wish we could do this more often,' he murmured, and she wondered if Laura would be as accepting as Lucy seemed to be, or if she would find it all too much. Were they making a mountain out of a molehill?

'Mum, I've got a call—I'll have the mobile if you need me, but could you keep an eye on Laura? It's likely to be a long delivery.'

'Sure. Have fun.'

Jo laughed. 'I doubt it somehow. It's in the forest, in a caravan—a traveller. I just hope nothing goes wrong. It's night-time, there's no power, no water, their neighbour's been done for GBH—it sounds brilliant.'

'Sounds as though she should be in hospital,' Rebecca said doubtfully.

'Tell me about it. She won't listen, and I can't withhold care on the strength of my opinion. Anyway, I'm off. See you later.'

'Have you got anyone with you?'

Jo laughed. 'Too right—I'm taking Ed. Nice and big and strong—he can carry water and keep the neighbours under control.'

She went out to her car and found Ed waiting, his bag at his side.

'Bringing your gear?'

'My obstetrics kit. You never know when you might need it. Jo?'

She met his eyes across the car. 'Yes?'

'Drive slowly—please?'

She laughed. 'You're safe, there's no rush. Get in.'

'Hmm.' He slid in beside her, folding up his long legs, and settled back against the seat. Bracing himself? Probably.

She drove carefully anyway because the roads were dark and a little slippery. It was quite mild, and it had rained earlier. A thin fog hung about the woods as they drove in, and she parked her car as far up the track as possible. Then they set off on foot.

Mel was walking around when they arrived, chanting a mantra with her eyes closed, and Andy was lying on the seat with the dog on his lap, watching her.

The dog growled, and Andy shushed him. 'Have a seat. She's doing her own thing at the moment. Want a cup of tea?'

'Yes, please. Hi, Mel,' she added, greeting the woman who had paused beside them and opened her eyes again.

'Hi. I'm trying to meditate through my contractions— it really seems to help.'

'How are you? What are they like—how often, how severe?'

'Oh, you know—one minute it's OK, and the next you think your legs are going to collapse. They're quite often now—Andy's timekeeping.'

'About every four minutes? They seem to last about a minute or so,' Andy offered.

Jo nodded. 'Right, can I have a look at you?'

'Sure.' She lay down on the bunk in the corner, and Jo felt around to check the presentation. 'Have your waters broken?'

'No—don't think so.'

'I think you'd know. Sometimes you can't tell, but usually it's pretty obvious. I'm going to examine you, see how far on you've got. Are you happy for Andy to be here?'

'Sure—and Ed. That's fine.'

Jo washed her hands, pulled on gloves and had a quick check to see how Mel's cervix was progressing.

'About six centimetres,' she said. 'That's good. You've got a while to go, but you're well under way. It's certainly not a false alarm.'

It was predictably slow, but with the conditions they were working under Jo was happier about that. It gave her time to feel her way through the labour, see if a pattern was emerging, check the contractions and make sure Mel was coping.

It was nearly four-thirty in the morning before Mel started to get too distressed, and then she stood up and headed for the door.

'I want to go outside, Andy,' she said.

'OK,' he agreed, and scooped up blankets, hurricane lights and a pillow.

'What?' Jo asked, stopping him with a hand on his arm. 'What's going on?'

'She wants to do this outside, in the forest. It's OK, I've built her a shelter. It's beautiful.'

Jo and Ed exchanged despairing glances, but there was no sense in arguing. Outside was as good as in so long as the presentation remained normal and Mel could cope. Her pelvic assessment had shown no evidence of disproportion, her baby was coming right on time, and they really had no justification for spoiling her delivery.

'I'll blow the whistle if necessary,' Jo said, and Ed nodded.

'OK. We'll go with it for now. She must be nuts, though, it's freezing.'

They followed the strange procession round to the other side of the caravan and inside what looked at first like a heap of branches. On closer inspection it was a three-sided shelter, with the open side facing east across a little clearing. There was a heap of bracken and heather piled up, and Andy laid blankets and quilts down over the bed to soften it for Mel.

She crawled in and lay on her side, panting and listening to the sounds of the night, the rustlings of the little animals, the hoot of an owl. It was beautiful, but perhaps not entirely practical.

Jo exchanged glances with Ed, and he shrugged. Go with it, he seemed to say. She checked Mel again, crawling into the shelter with her, and found that she was almost there.

'You're doing really well,' she told her. 'Just breathe through the last few contractions, and then you'll be in transition—can you remember about transition?'

Mel gave a wry grin. 'That's when I get crabby and tell you all to go to hell, isn't it?'

Jo laughed. 'Probably.'

'I want to get up,' Mel said suddenly. 'I want to walk round.'

'Andy, Ed, could you support her?' Jo asked, and they helped Mel out and walked her slowly round. She was doing fine until she came to push, and then she hung around Andy's neck. Jo spread a sheet of polythene over the forest floor under her, and she strained, and cried out, and panted, and strained again.

And nothing happened.

Ed looked at Jo. 'How's she doing?' he asked, crouching down beside her.

'Nearly crowning, but not progressing. Her pelvic floor's very strong.'

'Just push for me, Mel, one more time,' Jo coaxed.

'I can't,' Mel sobbed. 'I'm too tired. It hurts. I want my mum.'

'Oh, love,' Andy groaned. Shifting his grip, he hugged her, holding her up and supporting her. His muscles must be screaming, Jo thought, but he didn't for a moment suggest Mel should lie down.

Jo was struggling with the light of the hurricane lamp, and she wasn't happy. 'I need more light,' she said. 'Mel, I think you're going to have to lie down for a moment. Andy, can you lay her in the shelter? I want that inspection light you were talking about.'

It helped a little, but only to show her what she already knew. The baby was almost there, but stuck somehow.

'I wonder if it's a shoulder dystocia?' Ed murmured.

'I don't know. Her pelvic floor's so tight I can't tell, but that in itself shouldn't hold it up.'

'I'm not going to hospital,' Mel said desperately. 'I can't. Please, help me.'

'I just want to get something from my bag,' Ed said. 'Jo?'

She followed him round the other side of the caravan. The sky was lightening. At least, Jo thought, the ambulance won't have to find us in the dark.

'You want to take her in, don't you?'

Ed shrugged. 'It would be sensible, but I don't think she'll go and I'd like to try for her if I can. Episiotomy and another check?'

'If you like. Do you want to do it? At this point I'd probably call for help. She's been in the second stage for over an hour and got nowhere. What would you do in hospital?'

'For query dystocia? Episiotomy and ventouse, I think—more room and a little bit of suction probably. That's irrelevant. We haven't got the ventouse, and she needs help now. I don't want to hang about. I don't like the colour of that baby's head. I think it's getting distressed.'

'I'm happy to hand over to you,' Jo said, relieved that he was there and had so much obstetric experience. Up to now he'd been little more than back-up and an interested observer. Now, finally, she was able to lean on him—and he was there, with answers. 'Do whatever you want—I'll assist.'

Ed nodded. 'Right. I want to do a small cut, as much as anything so I can feel what's happening. Then I'll decide, but I've got forceps here if necessary. I don't suppose there's the slightest chance we can get her inside?'

Jo snorted. 'She's getting more stubborn by the minute. Let's just get the baby out. We can tidy her up anywhere later.'

'OK.'

They went back with Ed's bag, and explained what they were hoping to do.

'Oh, no! I want it naturally,' Mel sobbed. 'I knew it would be all instruments!'

'Mel, love, hush,' Andy pleaded. 'Listen to them.'

He calmed her while Ed gave her a local and then snipped carefully. The baby didn't advance at all and, putting one hand on her abdomen to press the baby down, he felt around its head with his other hand.

Mel gasped, and he apologised, but he kept on feeling, searching for that elusive something that was holding up the delivery.

'It's the anterior shoulder—it's hitched on the pubis symphysis—I'm going to try and push it back.'

'You're not lambing,' Jo said in his ear, and he chuckled drily.

'I noticed. Sheep are a damn sight easier. OK, Mel, just try and relax. That's it... No, I can't shift it. I want you on your hands and knees, and you're going to have to push like hell when I say so—all right?'

'I can't,' Mel sobbed. 'I want to die!'

'Rubbish. Come on, you can do it! Think of your baby,' Jo urged encouragingly, and they helped her onto her hands and knees.

Ed eased his hand in over the baby's head, lifting Mel's spine up away from the baby to expand her pelvis. He felt it give, felt the tiny shift in the baby's position, and then the surge of a contraction. 'OK, Mel, push!' he ordered, and lifted against her spine.

She did, dredging up a huge effort, and to his relief the baby slid forward. 'OK, stop pushing and pant— that's it, little breaths, good girl.' He eased his hand away, she pushed gently again, and the baby slithered into the world.

With a sob Mel collapsed against Andy and Ed scooped up the baby, flipped it over and checked it. He swept its mouth with his little finger, but it still didn't cry, and he didn't like its colour at all.

'It's flat—suction, please.'

Jo slipped a catheter into the infant's mouth and nose, sucking out the mucus in its airways. Then Ed clamped and cut the cord without ceremony, picked up the baby by its feet and swung it around.

'You should have been a vet,' Jo said in an undertone as the baby started to cry.

Ed grinned, checked it again and placed it on Mel's now-soft abdomen. 'Your baby,' he said gently, and she reached out and laid her hand over the baby's back.

'Hello, little one,' she murmured in wonder, and the first rays of the morning sun spilled over the horizon and turned her tears to gold...

'I'm sorry, but you can't stay here. You got your wish, and had the baby here, but you need several layers of sutures in that tear if you want to have a decent pelvic floor, and I can't do it with an inspection light. Ideally I'd want to do it with a general anaesthetic, but I'll compromise with you. You come to the GP unit and let me do it, and you won't have to go to the Audley and have a general. That's the choice.'

'Bully,' Mel said, but she was smiling at her baby. 'Can she come too?'

'Of course. I wouldn't dream of separating you. I'll get the ambulance to come for you now, and you can have some breakfast in there together and then we'll do it.'

Jo tidied up, packaging the clinical waste and sorting out the instruments, and wrote up notes. It had been nearly an hour since the baby was born, and they were back in the caravan in the warmth.

'I'll call the ambulance,' Ed said, and stepped outside into the lovely morning. A sound from his right caught his attention. Breaking glass? Something smashing?

'Sounds like Mick's having another trashing session,' Andy said, peering across the forest. 'He has a bad trip every now and again and goes berserk.'

They heard the sound of running footsteps, stumbling through the heather, and then Sioux burst into the clearing with blood streaming from her face, her baby clutched against her breast.

'Help me! He's going to kill me! Help me!'

Ed lobbed the phone at Jo. 'Call the police and an ambulance. Get them here now—fast. Tell them he's armed and dangerous.'

'Is he?'

'I don't know, but I wouldn't be surprised. And stay inside.'

He shoved Sioux through the door of the caravan, told

Andy to stay and guard them and, dropping down, zig-zagged through the forest. It had been years since his army training, but some things you never forgot.

Like bullies, and cruelty, and how to stay alive.

The smashing noise was coming from up ahead by Jo's car, and he slowed and peered round a tree. Mick was laying about the car with an iron bar, shattering the windows, smashing up the body panels—destroying it.

'Lying bitch!' he was yelling. 'I'll teach her to grass me up!' The headlights went, one after the other, and Ed waited. The car was wrecked. There was little more he could do to it but set light to it, and as long as he was here he wasn't near the women and children.

Ed wondered where the other men were, the ones from the other old coaches parked with his. Why didn't they do something to stop him? Were they all afraid, or didn't they think it was any of their business?

A groan from beside him attracted his attention, and he turned his head slightly. A man was lying in the heather, his face battered, his arm lying at a strange angle. Another victim?

Ed dropped onto his front and crawled across to the man. 'It's OK, I'm a doctor. Lie still, he's over there. Don't move.' He ran his eye over the man, noticing that although his clothes were casual, he wasn't dressed like the travellers.

'He'll kill Sioux,' the man whispered, grabbing Ed's arm in a surprisingly powerful grip. 'Stop him. He's dangerous.'

'It's OK, the police are coming. I can hear them.'

So could Mick. He threw down the iron bar, and ran towards one of the battered cars that lay around the fringes of the site.

Anger surged in Ed. There was no way he was going to get away. He ran after him, his legs pumping furiously, and tackled him just as he reached the car. They fell together into the dirt and rolled round, punching and kicking and struggling, until at last Ed found a purchase—the little tail of hair at the back of Mick's head.

He yanked it round, twisted him face-down into the sand and straddled him, kneeling on his arms.

'Don't move a bloody muscle,' he said viciously, 'or I'll beat you to a pulp.' He yanked the hair, just for good measure, and Mick gave a feeble scream and lay still. The sirens wailed to silence, and doors slammed.

'Over here,' Ed yelled. There was the sound of running footsteps and the police took over, handcuffing Mick and dragging him to his feet before leading him to one of the patrol cars.

The ambulance arrived—and then another one, for good measure.

'Excellent,' Ed said, dusting himself off and smiling grimly. 'Right, there's a man here with head injuries, a broken arm and possible internals, and a woman up the track with facial injuries and a baby that might have been chucked around a bit. I didn't have time to look. I suggest you take them both in one ambulance to the Audley, and then in the caravan up the way there's another woman with a new baby to go to the GP unit at Yoxburgh for postnatal care.'

'Busy night,' the ambulance driver said with a grin.

'Just a tad.'

He went with the ambulance to Mel's and Andy's caravan, and found Sioux still shaking uncontrollably.

'She's in shock. What's happened?' Jo asked.

'Police have got him.'

She looked at his filthy clothes in disbelief. 'What happened to you?'

'I was playing commandos,' he said with a grin.

'Action man, eh?'

He chuckled and hugged her. 'Something like that. Right, let's get this lot sorted out and have some breakfast—I'm starving.'

The police had to wait to interview Ed until Mel was stitched and comfortable. It turned out that the man he'd found by the car was Joe Saunders, the social services liaison officer who'd been trying to help Sioux.

'They've got a thing going between them, apparently,' Ed told Jo later that day at the surgery. 'Been going on for a few weeks.'

'Since I reported it to him. I hope he's all right.'

'I gather they are, all of them, and Mel had her dawn delivery.'

'You make it sound like the milkman,' Jo said with a laugh, then she sobered. 'You were wonderful. I don't know how you got that baby out.'

'Enormous skill—and brute force.'

Jo chuckled. 'Whatever, well done. And I gather you tackled Mick like something out of the SAS.'

'I was an army doctor,' he pointed out. 'That's where I did my obstetrics—on a military base in Germany. I learned a few sneaky tricks on the way.'

'Evidently.' She yawned hugely. 'I'm shattered. I'm going home to bed.'

'Lucky you. I've got an evening surgery. I'll see you tomorrow.'

'OK.' She hugged him. 'Thanks for your support. I couldn't have given Mel what she wanted without you.'

'Any sane person would have sent her to hospital, but maybe it's just as well we didn't or we wouldn't have been there to help the others.'

'And I might have had a car,' Jo said wryly.

'Look on the bright side—you get to choose a new one.'

'I liked it,' she said firmly. 'It was fun to drive.'

He groaned. 'Buy a milk float, for my sake.'

Jo snorted, and went home in the car she'd borrowed from her mother. She'd have to sort out a hire car tomorrow, but for now she was too tired to worry about it.

She went home, waved at everyone and went to bed, going out like a light. She woke the following morning, feeling heavy-eyed and sick.

Too much excitement, she thought, and sat on the edge of the bath, waiting for it to fill. The smell of burnt toast drifted up the stairs, and without any warning she felt a huge wave of nausea wash over her. She only just got her head over the loo in time.

Shaken, she washed her face and sat on the bathroom floor. Why was she feeling so sick? What had she eaten?

Nothing much. That might be the trouble. Perhaps she needed to eat something. The very idea turned her stomach, and she gulped in some air and stared at the ceiling. The last time she'd felt like this she'd been eighteen years old...

And pregnant.

CHAPTER TEN

JO WAS stunned. She couldn't be pregnant! Ed was sterile, he'd told her so—unless the effects of the chemotherapy had worn off and the sperm-producing cells had recovered.

Was that likely? Or, if not, was it at least possible? She consulted her books on infertility, and found nothing of any help or consequence. She carried the secret with her for the rest of the day until she could get into the surgery and do a pregnancy test. If she was right, and she was pregnant, she was sure Ed would be delighted.

Richard had been furious, but Ed loved children and had told her he'd like to have them with her. How wonderful it would be if they could have them naturally and not have to rely on technology to help them.

The test, when she found time to do it, was positive. She waited until Ed had finished his antenatal clinic, then slipped through the door.

'Have you got time to do one more quick antenatal check?' she asked him, bubbling over inside.

He glanced at his watch. 'Possibly. Who is it? Have you got the notes?'

She shook her head. 'No notes yet.' She drew a steadying breath. 'It's me.'

His head jerked up and he stared at her, then he gave a grunt of laughter. 'For a second there I thought you said it was you.'

'I did. It is.' She went over to him and stood by his chair. 'I'm pregnant, Ed,' she said, her happiness flowing over. 'We're going to have a baby.'

He stared at her for an age, hope warring with dis-belief, then he stood up and slammed his chair back against the wall, making her jump.

'How could you do that, Jo?' he said, his voice stran-gled.

'Do what?' she asked, stunned at his apparent anger. 'Don't you want a baby? I thought you wanted children. You said—'

'I know what I said.' He was staring out of the win-dow, his eyes wide and sightless, his voice ragged. 'Dear God, of all the ways to hurt me, why did you have to choose this one?'

She hurried to his side. 'Ed, no, listen! I really am pregnant. I'm having our baby—honestly! Ed, it's real. I've done a test. I'm about five and a half weeks—almost six.'

He turned and stared at her, but his eyes were icy cold and empty. 'So you might be, but not with my child, Jo. I'm sorry, you've picked the wrong man to try and fool. I know it isn't possible, and however desperate I might be to have children I'm not so desperate that I'll believe that.'

She gazed at him in disbelief. 'But, Ed—of course it's yours! Who else's could it be?'

'I don't know, you tell me,' he said harshly. 'How about Barry? Was it Barry? The groom in the panto? He fancies you—how do I know it's not him?'

'Of course it isn't! Don't be daft, he's a pillar of the local church! His wife did the costumes—his children were in the chorus! He is very definitely married!'

'So? So was Laura's father, and it didn't stop you last time—'

There was a sharp crack, and Jo felt the sting in her palm before she realised what she'd done.

'Bastard,' she whispered. 'You absolute bastard! How dare you?'

He stood motionless, not flickering so much as a muscle, and the perfect imprint of her hand slowly appeared on his cheek.

'You can deny it all you like,' he said distinctly, 'but if you're pregnant somebody else has got you that way. It isn't me and, OK, it may not be the guy in the panto, but you've been having an affair with someone, of that I'm sure.'

'In this community?' she raged. 'Do you really suppose, if I were having an affair with anyone else, that you wouldn't have heard about it?'

'Why should I?' he asked indifferently. 'No one knows about us.'

'Of course they do! Everyone knows! You can't do a damn thing in this town without a running commentary.' She rubbed her hand against her hip. Her palm was still stinging. God knows what his face felt like. She wasn't sure she cared at the moment.

'I'm going home. When you've calmed down and had time to think about it, perhaps you'd like to come and talk to me about how you suggest we tell Laura.'

'Tell her what you like,' he said coldly. 'It's nothing to do with me after all.'

'Ed, please, listen—'

'Just go, Jo. Get out of here, please, before I do something I'll regret.'

She searched his face and found no comfort, no compassion, no inkling of the love they'd shared. With a sob, she turned on her heel and ran...

Ed sat on the beach, miles along the coast from Dunwich, dropping pebbles in a little pile between his feet. His hands hung between his knees, his head was bowed and he felt sick.

He was gutted. After all she'd said, all the love they'd shared, the tenderness of their love-making…

A sob tore at his throat, and he clamped his jaws together and held it back. He wouldn't cry for her. She wasn't worth it. She was a liar, through and through.

He wondered how much of the story about Laura's father had been fabrication. All of it, probably. She'd probably had an affair with some spotty youth and got herself into trouble. Maybe she thought a married man sounded more grown-up, more interesting.

Oh, hell.

Well, she'd certainly had him fooled! He could have sworn she loved him, that she would have stood by him, but maybe all the talk about not pushing Laura was just an excuse to cool it? Maybe she'd got this other lover lined up, and Ed was just a convenient stop-gap if the other man was too busy…

He hurled a pebble out to sea, and then another, and another, until his little pile had vanished. Then he stood, dusted off the seat of his jeans and tramped back to the car. He had things to do—a house to find, for instance. He went into town, picked up a copy of the local rag and scanned it for property.

It was in the classified ads at the back—a property for renovation in an isolated setting on the edge of the forest.

Not everybody's cup of tea, but it would suit him down to the ground. He had money sitting waiting, he only had two weeks to find somewhere—this might just be the answer.

It was a private number, and the man offered to show him round that evening. He went, even though it was getting dark, and found the cottage on the road to the travellers' site, about half a mile this side of it. It was pretty, or could be, a little place with red brick and flint walls and a red pantiled roof set in a delightful little cottage garden, and he agreed a sale on the spot.

It took four days to do the deal—four days in which he kept the curtains closed at the back so he didn't have to look out over Jo's house, and harangued the solicitor mercilessly.

That evening he moved into his damp and chilly purchase, with its rotten window-frames and antiquated plumbing, the leaking roof and primitive kitchen. At last, in its peaceful surroundings, he found a place to lick his wounds.

'It seems strange without Ed in the cottage,' Rebecca said one evening as they were all sitting together in the drawing room.

Maurice was there, and Jo felt his eyes keenly on her.

'Yes, it is odd,' she said expressionlessly. 'Maurice, more coffee?'

'Thank you, my dear.' He passed his cup, watching her closely. 'I went and saw him at his new place over the weekend. It's very charming, I suppose, but it's rather tumbledown—needs a lot of work. Personally I wouldn't have thought it was fit to live in at the moment. It's near those travellers.'

'He should have stayed a little longer, and found himself a flat to move into, or a caravan to live in for a while. Heavens, Maurice, he could have moved back with you, or stayed here even! The cottage is free again after the Easter holidays. There was no need for him to rush into it. Most odd, if you ask me. Did he say anything to you, Jo?'

She shook her head. 'No, nothing. I think he just wanted to be independent.'

She sipped her glass of mineral water and tried not to notice the smell of the coffee, but all the time she could feel Maurice's eyes on her.

'Excuse me, I think I'll go and get on. I've got some notes to write up.'

'Before you go, dear, Maurice and I have got something to tell you both.' Rebecca reached out and took his hand, looking at him lovingly. 'He's asked me to marry him, and I've said yes.'

'That's wonderful,' Jo said with as much enthusiasm as she could muster. 'I'm really pleased for you both. I hope you'll be very happy together.'

'Laura?' Rebecca said, looking at her granddaughter in gentle reproach. 'Aren't you going to wish us well?'

'No—I don't want you to get married again! I want you here, with us! You're Grandad's wife, you can't marry him!'

And she leapt to her feet and ran out, sobbing.

Jo got up to follow. 'Mummy, I'm sorry, I'll talk to her—'

'No, I'll talk to her,' Rebecca said firmly. 'You stay here. I can deal with this better than you.'

She left the room, following the sound of Laura's running footsteps, and Maurice turned to Jo.

'When's it due?' he asked quietly.

'What?' She felt the colour drain from her face and sat again abruptly. 'I didn't hear you.'

'Yes, you did. It's Ed's, isn't it?'

She closed her eyes and nodded miserably. 'Yes. Yes, it is, but he doesn't believe it can be. He had testicular cancer twelve years ago, and the chemotherapy left him sterile, supposedly.'

'Only it hasn't.'

She gave a short laugh. 'You try telling him that. He thinks I've been having an affair with someone else.'

'Which, of course, you haven't. Oh, dear, what a shame. Do you love him very much?'

She nodded, fighting back the tears. 'Yes, I do. I thought he loved me too. He said he did, he even asked me to marry him, but Laura was so upset about you and Mum that we didn't like to spring anything else on her so we kept it quiet.'

'Upset? When was this?'

'A few weeks ago—the night you asked her to marry you. Laura saw you kiss her.'

A shadow crossed his face. 'Oh, dear,' he said heavily. 'I know how she adores her grandmother. Oh, blast, I wouldn't have hurt her for the world. And this happened at the same time?'

'Yes. Then I found out I was pregnant.'

'And that foolish boy doesn't believe it's his.' He shook his head. 'What a coil. I'll talk to him—'

'No. Don't bother. If he can't trust me and believe in me, he's not worth having. I just wish for his sake that he could believe it, because this child will grow up without him knowing he's the father, and that's so sad...'

She felt the warm, heavy comfort of Maurice's arm around her, and turned her head into his shoulder, allowing herself to cry at last. Then he mopped her up, fetched her another glass of water and sat down again.

'We were thinking... My house isn't in such good repair as this, so we wondered how you would feel about us living here. Then we'd be there for Laura—and we could help with the baby, too. I imagine you'll want to go on working?'

She shrugged helplessly. 'I don't know. I haven't got that far. I'm just getting through the days at the moment.'

'Well, think about it. Laura will come round. She just needs to accept that Graham's gone, then she'll be happier about Rebecca marrying me. It's a shock, too, discovering that your aged relatives have feelings and needs of their own. She needs time to come to terms with it.'

'And how will she feel about my needs and feelings when she finds I'm having a baby? I haven't even got a loving stepfather to present her with! What do I tell her—the stork brought it?' Jo shredded the tissue in her lap. 'She really adored Ed. They got on so well, he seemed really fond of her. Why won't he believe me?'

'Because it means too much? He's been told he could die. Then he's been told he won't die, but he won't have children. It's a sort of trade. He's clung to it all these years—presumably he's had other relationships and no one else has ever become pregnant. It would make it hard to believe you.'

'And, of course, it's easier to believe I'm a liar and a cheat.'

'Probably not. He looks like hell. If it's any consolation, I think he's desolate. He daren't believe you because there's too much at stake.'

She dropped her head into her hands. 'What am I going to do, Maurice? How can I convince him?'

'I could always persuade him to have a test. That would prove it.'

She lifted her head. 'Of course! That would show his sperm count had picked up—why didn't I think of that? Maurice, would you? Please?'

He reached out and patted her hand. 'I'll try. It may not work, but I'll do my best.'

Jo went to see Mel to check on her stitches and the progress of the baby, and passed Ed's car in the drive of a little cottage just off the road. So that was where he was living, she thought, and her heart ached. She drove right down the track this time, past the other settlement to Mel's caravan, and found Ed outside with Andy and the baby.

She got out, her heart pounding, and went over to them. 'Hi. Anything wrong?'

'No, just having a neighbourly chat,' Ed said distantly. 'I have to go. I've got a surgery in half an hour.'

He turned without a word to her and walked off across the heath in the direction of his cottage. Jo stifled a pang of grief and held her hands out to the baby. 'How is she today?' she asked, cuddling the little bundle.

'Fine. Mel's resting, she's been up at night a lot. The feeding's going really well.'

'Good.' She scraped up a smile and climbed up into the caravan. 'Hi, there. How are you feeling?'

'Tired, but OK. My tail's a bit sore. I've been sitting in a washing up bowl of salty water umpteen times a day, but it's still tender.'

'It will be. You ended up with a nasty tear, but at least the baby's all right. She's beautiful, you know.'

'I know. I'm so glad she was all right.'

Jo put her down. 'Can I feel how your tummy's going down?' she asked, and checked her patient quickly. She was recovering well, despite the unconventional surroundings, and Jo was pleased. The stitches had nearly all dissolved now, and the last couple she would take out the following day. She filled in her notes and propped the file back up behind the pan rack.

'Right, I'm off. I'll see you again tomorrow,' she said with a smile.

She went back to her car and drove down the track, and Ed was just pulling out of his cottage as she went past. He followed her all the way back to the surgery, haunting her rear-view mirror, and yet when they arrived he got out of his car, locked it and went in through the door without a word.

She might as well not have existed, she thought, and a great lump came up in her throat.

'Damn you, then,' she said quietly, and slammed the car door hard.

'Mr and Mrs Reynolds? What can I do for you?'

They were a couple in their late thirties, and they both looked drawn and worried, although it was Mrs Reynolds's notes Ed had in front of him.

'It's my wife,' Mr Reynolds said. 'She's been feeling off colour, and recently she's been having trouble with her waterworks—getting up and down all night, going every hour or so in the day, and, well, we can feel this lump over her bladder.'

Ed looked at the woman. 'Lump?' he said.

'Yes, a hard swelling. It doesn't hurt, but it presses.'

'Have you brought a urine sample?'

'Yes.' She fished a little pill-bottle out of her bag and handed it to him. It was impossible to see through the brown bottle so he put it down. He'd come back to it in a minute.

'I think I need to have a look at you. Could you slip your things off for me? I might need to examine you internally.'

He drew the curtains round the couch, and gave her a minute to undress while he asked the husband a few more questions about the onset of the problem and checked the urine in a clear bottle over the sink. It was normal in appearance, not cloudy or full of sediment, no streaks of blood or pus. He capped the bottle and washed his hands, then went behind the screen.

She was lying under the blanket, naked from the waist down, and he turned the blanket back and checked her abdomen. There was, indeed, a swelling just behind the pubic bone, but unless he was very much mistaken...

He pulled on a glove, squeezed a strip of lubricant on his fingers and gently inserted them, feeling for her uterus.

Idiot! If he'd been thinking clearly he'd have asked the question before, but he hadn't been. 'How are your periods?' he asked now.

'That's the other thing. I haven't had one for a while—not since before all this started.' She swallowed and summoned up her courage. 'Do you think I've got cancer of the uterus or bladder?' she asked with exaggerated calm.

He smiled wryly and stripped off the glove. 'No, I don't. I think, Mrs Reynolds, that you're going to have a baby—in about six months, at a guess. A scan will confirm the exact dates.'

'A baby?' she said incredulously, and sat up, swinging her legs over the side. 'But I can't be! We can't! Rob's sperm count's too low—we've been trying for fifteen years!'

And she burst into tears in her husband's arms.

Ed sat down with a bump. How ironic. Another faithless woman, cheating on her husband—but he, poor fool, was swallowing it hook, line and sinker.

'Well, I'm pretty sure,' he told them, summoning his professional calm. 'A test will confirm it, and then you'll need to make an appointment with one of the midwives—'

'Jo Halliday,' she said instantly. 'I've heard she's wonderful. Oh, I can't wait to tell my mother—she'll be thrilled for us! Oh, Rob, love!'

They hugged again, and Ed quickly dealt with the notes and sent them off with a test request. 'Just hand this in at Reception with your urine sample, and call back tomorrow for the result. Jo will see you as soon as it's confirmed and make arrangements to take over your care.'

Not that she'll be here at the end, he could have added, but it was up to Jo to sort that out. He couldn't be sure when her baby was due. All he could be sure of was that it wasn't his.

'We've been hoping for so long now we'd forgotten about it. Every month I used to wait for my period, and every month it used to come without fail, but after the tests we stopped worrying about it. I can't believe I didn't even think of it, but they were so negative when they did Rob's test we gave up hope then really. That was years ago.'

Jo couldn't believe what she was hearing.

'What did Dr Latimer say?' she asked.

'He just told me to get the result of the pregnancy test and then come and see you. He seemed pretty sure I was pregnant.'

Jo nodded. She'd been sure from her first look at the woman, but she wondered what Ed had made of the business of the low sperm count. Maybe this will convince him it's possible, she thought.

After her clinic Jo went to see if Ed was there, but he'd gone for the day. She went home, did some washing, helped Laura with her homework and then told her mother she had to go out on a visit.

It wasn't, strictly speaking, a lie. She was going to visit someone—just not a patient.

She headed slowly out into the forest and turned into Ed's drive, her heart in her mouth. His car was there, but there was no sign of him. She banged on the door, and light spilled down the hall from a room at the back. His firm tread approached, and the door swung inwards.

'What are you doing here?' he asked flatly.

'I wanted to talk to you.'

'I've got nothing to say.'

'But I have.'

He started to close the door but she blocked it and pushed her way in. She knew he wouldn't hurt her, no matter how hurt and angry he might be. 'Ed, please.'

He let go of the door and walked away, back down the hall to the light. She followed him, closing the door behind her, and found herself in a gloomy little kitchen. The plaster had been ripped off the walls, the wires dangled here and there, and the sink was propped up on a broom handle. 'What do you want?' he asked abruptly. 'I'm busy.'

She sighed, swept the plaster dust off a chair and sat down. 'Mrs Reynolds came to see me today.'

'Ah, yes—the immaculate conception. There's a lot of that about.'

She stared at him. 'What are you getting at?'

'Tell me,' he said with a humourless smile, 'do all the women in Yoxburgh cheat on their partners?'

'You don't have any trust in anyone, do you?' she said sadly. 'Not me, not Mrs Reynolds, not the rest of the pantomime cast—why can't you believe, Ed?'

He hit a section of plaster with a hammer and bolster, and it fell to the floor in a choking cloud of dust. 'Why should I? I know you're lying.'

'Why don't you have a test?' she suggested cautiously.

There was a crash, and the hammer fell to the floor on the other side of the room. 'Rather a pointless waste of resources, don't you think?'

'Absolutely, but since you won't believe me you obviously need proof.'

He picked up the hammer and attacked the wall again. She tried another angle. 'All right, then, if you won't have a sperm count, will you agree to a DNA test once the baby's born? That will prove paternity.'

He hit his thumb and swore viciously.

'Why don't you get the hell out of here and find some other sucker to bring up your baby, Jo? I'm not interested. Just give it up, for God's sake…'

His voice broke, and he dropped his head against the wall and dragged in a huge, unsteady breath.

'Oh, Ed,' she murmured, and stumbled through the rubble to his side.

'Don't touch me,' he bit out. 'Just go, Jo. Leave me alone. Stop torturing me.'

She stepped back. 'You're torturing yourself. If you'd only listen you'd be able to find out the truth, but you're too pig-headed to take anyone's word but your own. You want to be left alone? Fine! Well, I hope you rot in your miserable isolation. You deserve to!'

She turned and stumbled across the room. She tripped, going out into the hall, and banged her knee, but she scrambled up again and ran out, leaving the door open behind her. She could hardly see the road, and when she turned on the windscreen wipers it was no better.

With a broken sob she pulled over to the side of the road, rested her head on her arms and wept.

'I'm glad you could find time to come and see me. I've been talking to Jo,' Maurice said without preamble.

Ed's heart sank. Not him as well. He wondered why he'd been called into Maurice's consulting room after surgery.

'Maurice, it's between us. Leave it, please.'

'No, I won't leave it. This needs saying, and perhaps I'm the best person to say it. I've known Jo all her life. I've known her parents since before she was born, and I was the first person to know that she was expected.

I've also been her GP for the past thirty years, and I feel I have a knowledge of her that puts me in a unique position.'

Ed stared at his hands, his jaw set. 'What is your point, Maurice?'

'She's a dear girl—she's friendly, and jolly, and she makes friends easily—but she's nobody's fool. She was badly hurt twelve years ago—very badly hurt. She was devastated when she realised she was pregnant and the father wasn't interested. It's taken every one of those twelve years to screw up the courage to try again—and now that she has, because of your arrogant assumption that you couldn't possibly be wrong, she's going to have to bring up another child alone.'

Ed felt the tears threatening again. 'Maurice, it isn't arrogance,' he said roughly. 'I know it can't be mine—'

'Do you? When were you last tested? Twelve years ago, when you were twenty-odd? Smoking, drinking, sleeping with any woman that would have you, wearing tight jeans and snug little underpants? We've all been there, Ed. Isn't it possible that all of that might have affected your fertility?'

It was true, of course, every word. And it was possible that, over the years, his cells had recuperated a little.

Unlikely—but possible.

'Go and have a test, son. Don't do this to yourselves. I know that child's yours, just as I know the sun's going to rise tomorrow. You need to know it too.'

Maurice laid a heavy hand on Ed's shoulder and squeezed, then left him alone.

You need to know it too.

Ed reached for the phone, dialling automatically.

'So, this patient of yours is believed to have a low sperm count?'

Ed nodded, crushing his guilt for distorting the facts to his friend and one-time colleague.

'And they're having difficulty conceiving?'

'Um—well, not exactly. Apparently they have conceived—at least, she has. He doesn't believe it's his.'

Max straightened from the microscope he was peering into and shot back the seat. 'Well, he should. It could well be. Have a look.'

Ed stood slowly and went across to the microscope, bending to look into it. A handful of little tadpoles thrashed around in the light, wriggling furiously.

'So, are there enough there to do the business?' he asked a little unsteadily.

'Sure. It's a low count, true, but they're pretty fit little chaps.'

'So, given the right conditions...'

'Downhill with a following wind, yeah, why not? I wouldn't guarantee it, but people do the lottery every week for far worse odds. If I had that much chance of winning the lottery, I'd sell everything I owned to buy the tickets—and I'm not a gambling man.'

Ed watched the sperm for another minute, then straightened and met Max's altogether too perceptive eye.

'Thanks,' he muttered.

'Who is she?' Max asked gently.

There was no point in lying. 'Her name's Jo,' he said, and his voice sounded shaky.

'You love her, don't you?'

Ed nodded. His eyes were prickling again, and he looked down at his hands. 'Yes, I love her. I might have burnt my boats, though.'

Max's hand landed on his shoulder. 'You'd better go and find out, then, hadn't you?'

*   *   *

The door of the cottage opened quietly, and Jo came to the top of the stairs. 'Mum?' she called.

There was no reply. She started down, just as Ed appeared at the foot of the stairs. He looked defeated.

'Can I talk to you, please?' he said quietly.

'Now? I'm busy. We've got guests tomorrow—'

'It won't wait.'

She came down the stairs a little. 'OK. We'll go to the house—'

'No, here. There's no one here, is there?'

'No.' She sat down on the step, and he climbed the stairs and sat beside her, his leg resting against hers, his shoulder beside hers. He looked awful.

'I've been to see a friend who's got a lab,' he began.

'And?'

'I owe you an apology. You were right. My sperm count's picked up. It's not good, but it's good enough—just.'

Jo felt a huge pain in the region of her heart, and she lashed out. 'So, because this friend says it's OK, you're going to believe me now, are you?'

'I always wanted to believe you,' Ed said, his voice low and ragged. 'For a moment, when you told me, I almost let myself, but I've known for so long that it wasn't possible—if it had been, it would have happened before now. Victoria didn't become pregnant, and we weren't taking any steps to prevent it. We were together for two years. If it had been possible, it would have happened then.'

'Maybe we were just very lucky, if that's the word,' Jo suggested bitterly. 'I'd just ovulated—I know that because I get a little pain sometimes. Perhaps we just hit it right.'

'Downhill with a following wind,' he said softly.

She looked at him in surprise. 'Something like that.

Anyway, that's beside the point. The real issue here is that you didn't trust me. You couldn't believe in me. Do you have any idea how much that hurts?'

Her voice broke, and she felt Ed's arm hover uncertainly around her shoulder for a moment. Then, with a ragged groan, he drew her into his arms. 'Don't,' he said unevenly. 'Jo, don't. I never meant to hurt you. I'd die before I could willingly hurt you—'

'You were so cruel—'

'I know. I knew it couldn't be mine, and there was only one other way. The thought of some other man touching you, loving you the way I had—it hurt so much I lashed out. I can't tell you how sorry I am. I wanted to trust you, but I don't believe in miracles. It meant so much to me, and it seemed like such a cruel twist of fate.' He bowed his head. 'Forgive me, Jo—please? Let's start again.'

She felt the pain in her heart disintegrate. So he'd hurt her, but only because he'd been so hurt in the past. She stood up and held out her hand to him, drawing him to his feet.

'Can we?' she whispered. 'I've missed you so much.'

His eyes searched her face incredulously, and then with a cry he swept her up into his arms and hugged her tight. 'Oh, Jo, I've missed you, too. I thought I'd die without you. The thought of the rest of my life without you was unbearable.'

His lips found hers, and he kissed her tenderly, almost reverently. 'I love you,' he whispered against her hair. 'Marry me.'

She leaned back in his arms and smiled. 'Haven't you forgotten something?' she teased.

He smiled back. 'Marry me *now*?' he asked, and then his voice cracked. 'Marry me—please?'

'I should be honoured,' she said gently, and lifted her face to his kiss...

EPILOGUE

'HE'S gorgeous.'

Jo looked down at the baby in her arms and smiled. 'Mmm—just like his father.'

Sue propped her arms on the edge of the crib and laughed softly. 'You're biased.'

'Of course.' Little Thomas was asleep now, his rose-bud mouth soft around her nipple. She eased him away and handed him to Sue while she fastened her clothes, but he started to grizzle so she took him back again as soon as she was done. 'Let's go back down to the others. We can't abandon them.'

'It's been a lovely christening—what a good idea to combine it with the house-warming.'

Jo laughed mirthlessly. 'It's been hell—what are you talking about? The place was in chaos until yesterday.'

Sue looked around the hall as they joined the others. 'Well, it looks wonderful now.'

'Doesn't it, just?' Maurice said, glancing around the sitting room of his old home. 'I hardly recognise it. I must say I think you've done wonders—it was a very old-fashioned sort of house when I lived here.'

Ed laughed. 'It was a lovely home—but anything we've done we have Andy to thank for. He's been fantastic.'

'And Mel—the curtains are all hers. She's done a wonderful job.'

'Don't, we'll get swollen-headed,' Mel said with a chuckle. 'I think I'm going to have a holiday now—

perhaps we'll have time to get back to work on our house.'

Ed gave a rueful grin. 'Sorry—it was a bit much to sell it to you in that state and then ask you to help with this straight away.'

'No problem. Just put our name about, that's all,' Andy said with a smile. He shifted his little daughter to the other arm, and she reached out to touch Thomas's head.

'He's cute,' Mel said.

'He's my baby brother,' Laura said proudly. 'D'y'know, I really wanted a sister, but he's so nice I love him to death. Anyway, we'll be able to play football, won't we, sport?'

'Maybe next time,' Jo said, exchanging glances with her mother.

Rebecca gave a secretive smile and turned away. 'Come on, Maurice, I want to show you what they've done out here in the kitchen. We might try something similar in our new house.'

Ed and Jo wandered through their guests, laughing and chatting, and then by a miracle found themselves alone in the conservatory at the back. Early geraniums bloomed in pots, and it was leafy and cosy and private.

'Are you all right?' he asked her softly. 'Not too tired?'

'I'm fine. You?'

He smiled tenderly at her. 'Just counting my blessings. I can't believe how everything's worked out in the last year. You know, when I met you, I thought how wonderful it would be if I could persuade you to marry me. You'd already had a baby so I didn't feel I'd be cheating you if things didn't work out—and then Thomas appeared on the scene.'

'It was a bit early—I've often wondered if you would have liked more time before starting our family.'

He shook his head. 'No. There's only one thing I'd change, and you know what that is.'

'I've forgiven you for that,' she told him softly.

'I haven't. I'll never forgive myself for doubting you—and the more I know you, the more I realise how much it must have hurt.'

'Forget it. It's over, Ed. I love you.'

'I love you too. I loved you anyway. Spending my life with you would have been more than reward enough. To have Laura and Thomas as well—it's just an unexpected bonus.'

She smiled and handed him his son. 'You think he's such a bonus—you change his nappy.'

Ed grimaced. 'Thanks.'

'My pleasure. You'd better get used to it. I'll need your help more than ever when the next one comes along.'

'If it does. Let's not count our chickens before they're hatched.'

'I'm not. I'm counting our blessings—and at the last count there was one more on the horizon. You're getting another bonus, Dr Latimer.'

He stared at her, not quite able to believe his ears. 'What?' he said weakly.

She smiled. 'Downhill, with a following wind...'

He closed his eyes and reached for her. 'Wow,' he said softly. 'It's a good job we bought this big house off Maurice. Looks like we're going to need lots of room.'

'Mmm. We'll be supplying the whole of the junior chorus in the panto at this rate. *Babes in the Wood* might be appropriate.'

'Just so long as we don't do *Ali Baba and the Forty Thieves*!'

MILLS & BOON®

*M*akes
any time
special

Enjoy a romantic novel from
Mills & Boon®

Presents™ Enchanted™ Temptation®

Historical Romance™ Medical Romance™

MILLS & BOON®

Medical Romance™

COMING NEXT MONTH

VILLAGE PARTNERS by Laura MacDonald

Dr Sara Denton tried to forget Dr Alex Mason, but it didn't work. Then she went to her uncle's and found Alex was a partner at the general practice! And Alex *really* wanted her to stay…

ONE OF A KIND by Alison Roberts

Dr Sam Marshall, fresh from Australia, was certainly unique! Sister Kate Campbell, with an A&E department to run at the busy London hospital, had no time to spare, but Sam was persistent!

MARRYING HER PARTNER by Jennifer Taylor
A Country Practice—the first of four books.

Dr Elizabeth Allen wasn't comfortable with change, but when Dr James Sinclair arrived at the Lake District practice, change was inevitable!

ONE OF THE FAMILY by Meredith Webber

Nurse Sarah Tremaine wanted to adopt baby Sam, but first she had to get permission from the child's uncle. But Dr Adam Fletcher didn't know he had a nephew…

Available from 7th May 1999

MILLS & BOON®

Next Month's Romance Titles

♡

Each month you can choose from a wide variety of romance novels from Mills & Boon®. Below are the new titles to look out for next month from the Presents™ and Enchanted™ series.

Presents™

THE SPANISH GROOM	Lynne Graham
HER GUILTY SECRET	Anne Mather
THE PATERNITY AFFAIR	Robyn Donald
MARRIAGE ON THE EDGE	Sandra Marton
THE UNEXPECTED BABY	Diana Hamilton
VIRGIN MISTRESS	Kay Thorpe
MAKESHIFT MARRIAGE	Daphne Clair
SATURDAY'S BRIDE	Kate Walker

Enchanted™

AN INNOCENT BRIDE	Betty Neels
NELL'S COWBOY	Debbie Macomber
DADDY AND DAUGHTERS	Barbara McMahon
MARRYING WILLIAM	Trisha David
HIS GIRL MONDAY TO FRIDAY	Linda Miles
BRIDE INCLUDED	Janelle Denison
OUTBACK WIFE AND MOTHER	Barbara Hannay
HAVE BABY, WILL MARRY	Christie Ridgway

On sale from 7th May 1999

H1 9904

Available at most branches of WH Smith, Tesco, Asda, Martins, Borders, Easons, Volume One/James Thin and most good paperback bookshops

R.J. KAISER

Easy Virtue

A showgirl, a minister and an unsolved murder!

When her father was convicted of a violent murder she knew he didn't commit, Mary Margaret vowed to clear his name. She joins forces with Reverend Dane Barrett, and bit by bit they uncover the veil of mystery surrounding her father's case—enough to clear his name and expose the real killer.

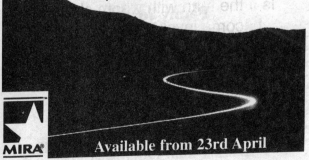

2 FREE
books and a surprise gift!

We would like to take this opportunity to thank you for reading this Mills & Boon® book by offering you the chance to take TWO more specially selected titles from the Medical Romance™ series absolutely FREE! We're also making this offer to introduce you to the benefits of the Reader Service™—

- ★ FREE home delivery
- ★ FREE gifts and competitions
- ★ FREE monthly Newsletter
- ★ Exclusive Reader Service discounts
- ★ Books available before they're in the shops

Accepting these FREE books and gift places you under no obligation to buy, you may cancel at any time, even after receiving your free shipment. Simply complete your details below and return the entire page to the address below. *You don't even need a stamp!*

YES! Please send me 2 free Medical Romance books and a surprise gift. I understand that unless you hear from me, I will receive 4 superb new titles every month for just £2.40 each, postage and packing free. I am under no obligation to purchase any books and may cancel my subscription at any time. The free books and gift will be mine to keep in any case.

M9EA

Ms/Mrs/Miss/Mr .... Initials ....

BLOCK CAPITALS PLEASE

Surname ....

Address ....

....

.... Postcode ....

Send this whole page to:
THE READER SERVICE, FREEPOST CN81, CROYDON, CR9 3WZ
(Eire readers please send coupon to: P.O. BOX 4546, DUBLIN 24.)

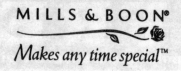

MILLS & BOON®

Makes any time special™

The Regency Collection

Mills & Boon® is delighted to bring back, for a limited period, 12 of our favourite Regency Romances for you to enjoy.

These special books will be available for you to collect each month from May, and with two full-length Historical Romance™ novels in each volume they are great value at only £4.99.

Volume One available from 7th May